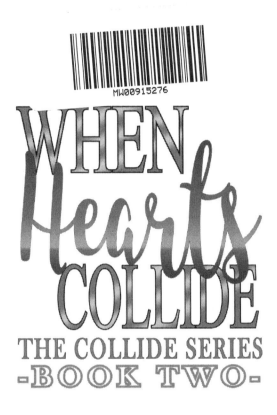

WHEN Hearts COLLIDE

THE COLLIDE SERIES
-BOOK TWO-

A Trilogy by Millie Belizaire

MillieBelizaire.com

Edited by **Christina D.**
Cover Designed by **Millie Belizaire**
eBook Formatting by **Millie Belizaire**

Table of Contents

TABLE OF CONTENTS   3

AUTHOR'S NOTE   6

CHAPTER ONE   7

CHAPTER TWO   13

CHAPTER THREE   25

CHAPTER FOUR   45

CHAPTER FIVE   58

CHAPTER SIX   82

CHAPTER SEVEN   90

CHAPTER EIGHT   97

CHAPTER NINE   108

CHAPTER TEN   122

CHAPTER ELEVEN   131

CHAPTER TWELVE   139

CHAPTER THIRTEEN   147

CHAPTER FOURTEEN   158

CHAPTER FIFTEEN   168

CHAPTER SIXTEEN   **175**

CHAPTER SEVENTEEN   **183**

CHAPTER EIGHTEEN   **191**

Author's Note

Thank you for reading. I hope you leave a review (:

Chapter One

KAIN

I don't believe in luck.

In life, if something is going to happen, it will certainly happen. People who sit around on their asses waiting for things like luck to interfere deserve whatever fucked up situation that way of thinking puts them in. For someone who didn't believe in luck—for a while, I'd been feeling quite lucky. I'd met a girl who brightened my days, and for a suspiciously long time, life felt like a dream.

Lauren.

I was with her the night reality finally came knocking at my door. Reality, if nothing else, is ridiculously reliable. It always comes back. It always shows up, an ultimatum never too far behind.

My options were simple; it was do or die.

And in so many words, Lauren had practically asked me to leave my decision up to luck. I couldn't say I was surprised that she was the type to hold out hope for divine intervention. Enough bad things hadn't happened to her for her to realize that *this*—this was real life.

And in life, if something is going to happen, it will certainly happen. And the only thing that you can count on interfering is yourself.

"Lauren!" I didn't like yelling at her, but she made it so hard not to in that moment. "I can't do this with you right now."

There was a short back and forth—a waste of time, really—before she ultimately swallowed hard, her eyes flooded with tears. As if it were the last thing she had left, she said *the* words.

"I love you. Please don't go. I love you."

I hated the fact that my heart responded to the confession. In any other scenario, those words were something that I would've wanted to hear. They would've meant something to me. However, they couldn't right now. Part of me was angry that she would weaponize love, of all things. Was I supposed to change my mind and let Amir die because she loved me? Is that what she thought would happen?

* * *

With so much going on in my mind, I couldn't afford to think about what I'd said to Lauren. Yes, I felt guilty, but I did what needed to be done. I couldn't take back what I said, but I could sooner ask for Lauren forgiveness than bring Amir back from the dead.

So I made a decision and broke her heart.

I promised myself that I would apologize for it later.

It was raining that night, so of course, the Saturday night traffic was extra thick. I didn't have a plan. I didn't even have hope. I just knew I had to try. All my sister had in her car's glove compartment was a switchblade. With no backup and no gun, I was, without a doubt, walking into a suicide mission. But this was Amir we were talking about here. I didn't have a choice.

I took the blade with me, leaving the car parked on the sidewalk in front of the club.

There was a sea of people rushing out of *Poseidon* when I arrived on the scene. Amidst the screaming, I could very clearly make out the popping sound of gunshots. Before that night, I had never ended anyone's life. It was actually kind of an accomplishment considering the world I'd grown up in. The people in my life had stories for days about their very first kills. I was once told that some people don't find out that they're not cut out for killing until after the deed is done.

They fire one bullet, see the damage caused, and just panic. They find it difficult to cope with the reality that they took a life. Some people are just not born to kill others.

I wondered if maybe that would be me.

Not gonna lie, part of me had already come to the conclusion that it wouldn't be.

As a crowd spilled out from inside the glass-walled club, I was running in the opposite direction, going towards the gunshots instead of away from them. No one was paying attention to me amidst the chaos, however, not while the inside of the club sounded like a Middle East war zone.

I was expecting five gunmen, but I only counted three. My eyes zeroed in on the one standing furthest from the other two, his eyes scanning the crowd for—*me*, probably.

That's who they were here for.

Me.

I ducked my head in, looking for blind spots. I needed to get my hands on his gun and to do that without getting shot, I needed to be discrete about it. The other two gunmen shot sporadically into the panicking crowd. It was with disgust that I noted that although they'd come to the club for me, they were still unleashing a rain of bullets unto an unsuspecting crowd—killing them because they could.

While the other two were occupied with their sick game of senseless murder, I pulled the blade out of its casing with my teeth, coming up behind the lone gunman, knife risen toward his neck. In one swift motion, the cut was deep, sending a stream of blood cascading down his shirt, his hands coming up to his neck as if to stop himself from choking on his own blood.

When he fell, the gun fell with him. His eyes were still open. I couldn't tell if he died that way, or if I would be the last person this man ever saw. I didn't lean down to check his pulse. No, I only bent to pick up his gun. I'd just killed a man with a switchblade and the only thing I could think about doing next was counting the bullets in this gun so I would know if I had enough to kill the next four.

Not a lick of remorse. To my disappointment, I was killing with ease.

I counted two bullets.

Shit.

Two bullets. Four gunmen. No backup.

I stepped around the mirrored tables surrounding me, careful not to step on any of the bodies on the ground. The two gunmen at the opposite end of the club continued to fire rounds into a screaming crowd, nodding to one another as though they were on a successful hunting trip. I crept in closer, closing one eye so I could get in a clear shot. When I felt precise enough, I pulled the trigger, hitting one of the murderous duo right between the eyebrows.

One bullet. Three gunmen. No backup.

"I found him! He's in here!" The second gunman fired erratically, half a dozen shots levied in my direction. A bullet narrowly missed my neck. I actually felt its heat as it passed a fraction of a centimeter away from my skin. "Yoooo, by the bar! It's Ka—"

Two gunmen left. No backup. No bullets.

If I had moved a second slower when I jumped behind the bar, I would have caught at least four bullets. The sounds of gunfire did not let up. The two remaining gunmen fully stepped out from the back and fired into the wood of the bar. I could feel the shots vibrating the furniture against my back. In front of me, bottles of liquor shattered, caught in the line of fire, splashing alcohol everywhere, soaking my clothes.

I looked around me for a weapon, an idea—*something*. The only thing my eyes fell on was the lifeless body of a Poseidon bartender, crouched behind the bar counter beside me. That would be me soon enough.

I'm fucked.

I focused on the sound of the approaching gunshots. At that moment, I didn't think about myself, I didn't think about Amir. I thought about the pain I'd left in her eyes, and how regretful it was that I wouldn't get a chance to say I was sorry.

And then the gunfire ceased.

For a minute, I didn't move, unsure if this was just some ploy to get me to step away from what was shielding me.

"Ayo, Youngblood! Ayo, Youngblood! That you behind the bar?"

With a shake of my head, my shoulders relaxed, the speed of my heartbeat slowing. Backup had finally arrived.

Youngblood.

No one had called me that in over twelve years.

Chapter Two

KAIN

They were calling it The *Poseidon* Massacre.

It was just like the news media to give some real shit a Hollywood-ass title. But honestly, it all kind of did feel like a movie. At times, the levels of sensationalism were almost too much to take seriously. News networks were making fools of themselves, spinning narratives and theories that couldn't have been further from the truth.

CNN was using the tragedy as a springboard to launch into conversations about gun control.

MSNBC was spinning conspiracy theories about it being some mystery gang shootout.

FOX News wanted to make it about Islam so bad.

None of it was real. The reporters knew just as much as everyone else. Nothing.

The sheer volume of lives lost had turned The *Poseidon* Massacre into an ongoing FBI investigation. What happened at *Poseidon* was now a full-on federal case.

But the feds didn't know shit either.

The case would go cold in less than a year, and the families of those who died would just have to deal with that. They would probably never get closure. *Oh, fuckin' well...*

My family *does not* cooperate with the police. We deal with our enemies on our own terms. If somebody needs to get punished, we don't wait for court cases and trials.

Strange as it seems, I might've forgiven Lyle and Rochelle for trying to kill me. It made sense. My father killed their son, so it was only natural for them to want me dead in retaliation. I could forgive transgressions done in the name of revenge. Revenge is a natural and human motive.

But they didn't fucking kill me.

So all that extra shit... It was for nothing. Seventy-two random people, and my best friend, died for *nothing*. Somebody get on FOX News and tell them *that* shit!

Those lost at *Poseidon* were all just collateral damage in an otherwise failed mission. Every single last one of them. *Meaningless*.

I was in Memphis.

The city was unfamiliar to me. Last time I was here was for my grandmother's funeral. I think I was thirteen. Memphis had always been a city of death for me. Not because I found it particularly dangerous, but because the only time I ever paid a visit, somebody in the family was being put in the ground.

"You a'ight, Kain?"

Silas was practically breathing down my neck. The old man was all too eager to get this over with, and I was tired. Not physically tired. I'd slept the whole three-hour private flight. I think I was emotionally exhausted. My mind felt drained, and it felt like I was seeing the world around me with slightly duller coloring.

"I'm good," I assured, "Where is she?"

Silas lead the way, his arm stretching out ahead of us as he walked me down into the basement of our Memphis home.

God, I really hate this place, I thought to myself as I passed pictures of me from my childhood hanging from the wall. My grandmother used to live here when she was alive. Without her here, this house just felt like an empty shell.

And here I was, ready to besmirch grandma's house with bloodshed.

As Silas lead me further into the basement, the sounds of heavy breathing echoed throughout the concrete room, bouncing off the solid gray walls. Soon Rochelle came into view, her slender stature crumpled into a corner, her breathing erratic. No one bothered tying her up or handcuffing her to anything. She'd been badly beaten, and I was sure she *couldn't* walk up the stairs and out of this house even if given the chance.

"Hey, Auntie Ro."

Old habits die hard. I was so used to calling her that, that it didn't even feel strange until after I had time to really think about it. I was here to kill her. Yet I still called her Auntie Ro. Tragic.

Rochelle would be my fourth body in two days.

Last night at *Poseidon*, I had managed to pick off three of the five gunmen on my own before back up arrived. Still, the three men from last night didn't mean anything. I didn't know their stories. I didn't even know their names.

But I knew Rochelle. She was family—by marriage, but still family.

Silas had killed her husband not long before I arrived, his own brother. I suppose he wanted desperately to kill Rochelle himself as well, but he saved her for me.

Saved her for me.

Sick.

But I wasn't complaining. I wanted her.

Anyone who's ever paid attention would know that The *Poseidon* Massacre was all Rochelle. Lyle didn't have the heart (or lack of it) to pull off a stunt like that. Only Rochelle was calculated enough, smart enough, and batshit crazy enough to do something like this. The gunmen last night had been members of *her* family, going all out to avenge the death of her son.

I wondered what the news networks would say to that. The deadliest mass shooting in American history was orchestrated by a devastated mother, putting everything on the line in the name of revenge.

That's some Hollywood shit, ain't it?

The gun in my hand raised and stopped between Rochelle's brows.

"It wasn't about you, Kain," she whispered, tears pooling over from her reddened eyes. I drew the gun back, reaching into my back pocket for the silencer. "It wasn't about you," she repeated.

I understood. Everything she did was about getting back at Silas.

Softly, I replied, "I know." Images of last night flashed through my memory as I screwed the silencer onto the gun. "What I'm about to do ain't about you either, Ro." I pulled my thumb over the gun's safety latch, cocking it once before positioning it between her eyes. This was about the brother I'd lost last night. "This is for Amir."

My family does not cooperate with the police. We deal with our enemies on our own terms.

And for that reason, I pulled the trigger.

The days meshed together into one long night. I couldn't be sure if the sun was up or down from the way I kept the blinds drawn throughout the house.

Silas was still in Memphis, finishing off any and everyone who was in on Rochelle's scheme. At this point, he was just doing this to save face. If Silas didn't go all out with this tour of retribution, niggas wouldn't think twice about crossing him in the future.

My father's rampage throughout his hometown was now less about revenge and more about getting a message across.

If anyone bothered to ask me, I would have said he was overdoing it. But then again, I was too exhausted to ever be as thorough as Silas. *Exhausted as hell.*

Getting back into my old habits, I had been having trouble sleeping.

In a moment of desperation, I'd driven to Pembroke Pines in the hopes that I might finally be able to sleep if it was in the bed Lauren and I had once shared. Sleeping in that house had always been easy. It felt like home.

Going there only made the sleeplessness worse. I lied wide awake that night, reliving memories and conversations with a woman that felt worlds away.

The *fucking* pillows smelled like her hair.

I didn't sleep a wink. An unsurprising truth hit me as the sun rose and began to shine into that empty bedroom.

It wasn't the house that felt like home. It never was.

It was her.

If I stayed there, I might've never gone back to sleep. So I took my ass back to the big house after that. Aside from Vance, everyone in this house knew to leave me alone. This was not because I'd given Vance any kind of special permission. Vance just didn't give a shit about my boundaries.

It was day six since The *Poseidon* Massacre. *#PrayForMiami* was still trending all over the internet. I was in the living room flicking between the three major news networks.

"You gon' stay on the news for the rest of your life, Youngblood?"

I tossed Vance a look from where I sat on the couch. *Leave me alone*, it said.

Vance looked like he might say something else to annoy me, but he was cut off by the sound of the doorbell. It was almost midnight.

"That for you?" I asked. I wasn't expecting anyone.

Vance shot me a grimace, almost rolling his eyes at the stupid question. "Yeah, kid, I've made *lots* of friends since I got out of prison last week."

I almost smiled at his sarcasm, but the response was also kind of sad.

The doorbell sounded three more times in rapid succession.

"You not gon' get that?" Vance asked me.

"I don't answer doors for people who don't call first." The live-in staff was off the clock, so whoever was at the door was not getting in.

Vance chuckled at this, walking further into the living room and snatching the remote out of my hand. "Which channel is it for the security cameras?"

"Switch to the HDMI 3 output," I replied. The doorbell sounded two more times before Vance pulled the security camera feed onto the living room television.

When I saw who was at the door, something in my stomach dropped.

How the fuck...?

"Hmm…" Vance squinted, moving closer toward the big screen to get a better look. Changing my tune, I was already rising to my feet. That was when the banging started. "*Shiiiiiit*, back in my day niggas got shot for bangin' on people's doors like that."

"They still do," was all I said as I cut across the kitchen and headed for the house's main door. It took a lot of restraint to not rush frantically to open it. It took even more restraint to keep a straight face as it opened.

I comfortably leaned against the doorframe, my nonchalant body language the complete opposite of what was swimming around in my head. In my mind, I was losing my shit.

Lauren.

Not a lick of emotion crossed my features as I looked her over. I made sure of it.

Still, I noted everything that was wrong immediately. She had been crying. The white tank top that she had on was dirty like she'd been pushed into the dirt. There were scratches on her arms and hands. Across her left cheek was a visibly deep purple bruise, blemishing her dark brown skin.

Something in my chest tightened at the realization that she'd been hit—hard.

Keep a straight face.

Lauren's eyes met mine and something in my stomach twisted. Like me, she knew not to wear her reaction on her face. *Of course. My baby is smart.* Her dark eyes were depthless, almost soulless. Was that an act? Or did someone really break her? Did they do that?

Or was it me?

My eyes scanned over the rest of her body, settling at her upper arm where the hand of some nigga was clutching her way too fucking tight. It was a territorial type of hold, like he really thought he owned her. My jaw clenched.

Keep a straight face, I reminded, just before promising myself that I was gonna break that hand before the night was over.

"Yo, you Kain, right?" I was asked this question by the man who didn't have his hands on my girl. I squinted at the stupid question. Who the fuck else would I be? "Yeah, yeah…" he answered his own question. "I thought you were."

Both men were about my age, if not two or three years older. I guess that's why the one who was digging his nails into Lauren thought he could call me—

"*Bruh*," he exclaimed. "The state attorney's daughter—we *got* her."

I didn't like the way he said that shit. Lauren is a person, not a sports fish.

Rather harshly, he shoved my girl further into the light. Lauren winced ever so slightly, pained by the roughness of his movements. I could feel the muscle between my eyebrows twitch involuntarily. Once she was in the light adequately enough, he finally let her arm go, inviting me to take a look for myself.

All I could see was the disregard he had for her body. The indents of his fingernails had settled into her skin. There would be bruises and scabs tomorrow morning. I reached out, my hand brushing against the superficial cuts. Under the feel of my touch, I could sense her body grow a little less tense.

That's right, baby. You're safe.

Tucking a finger under her chin, I raised her head to bring her eyes to mine. I searched for answers in them. *Baby, what did they do to you?*

It was almost painful to have to look away. They didn't catch the true meaning of my actions. The last thing anyone would expect was that Lauren Alyssa Caplan was mine. The last thing anyone would expect was that I was hers, too. I didn't even think she fully realized that second truth herself.

"I'm Jerome," the handsy one introduced himself, and then pointed to the man behind him. "This is my partner, Grip."

When I finally spoke, my tone was natural. I had learned to not let my emotions affect my exterior a long time ago.

"And?"

He puffed out his chest, not liking my dismissive tone.

"And we the niggas that got her, know what I'm sayin'?" he asserted as if to say until I paid the bounty, Lauren still belonged to them. To further drive his point, he reached out to grab her. As a reflex, she cringed away from his hands, crashing into my chest. My arm came around and swiveled her behind me.

With Lauren out of his reach, Jerome pointed at her and shouted, "You ain't paid for her yet!"

Who the fuck does this nigga think he's shouting at?

I straightened up at the sound of that disrespectful ass tone, my eyes daring him to rethink his approach. If he wanted to make power moves, he'd better be able to back that shit up. Jerome took a step back, patting his waistband as a reflex. I recognized the impulse well—he was feeling for his gun. Bitch made individuals always feel for their guns before they need to, thinking that it comes off as hard when they let niggas know they're carrying.

The gesture didn't disturb me in the slightest. "Try me."

His partner tried to cut into the tension. "Look, we don't want no problems, Kain. We'd just like to speak to Silas about that money we 'posed to get for her."

"Silas ain't here."

"Then we can come back with her when he is," Jerome remarked. He extended a hand, beckoning for Lauren to come back. When she didn't move, he promised, "I swear I won't let Grip touch you again."

Again.

My eyes darted to the lanky nigga standing behind Jerome. I must've forgotten to keep a straight face because he took one look at my expression and moved three steps back. Nodding to myself, I broke the silence.

"What was it—two hundred thousand?"

Jerome relaxed, solaced by the promise of money, hope in his tone when he replied, "Yeah. Two hundred Gs."

"I've got your money," I disclosed.

Over my shoulder, I glanced at Lauren and motioned for her to take several paces back. Once she was sufficiently out of the way, I stepped aside and nodded the two men inside. I watched them think about it for maybe a second, ignoring the warning signs, blinded by money. They didn't even hesitate as they crossed the threshold, and into the house.

In truth, I had no intention of shelling out any kind of money for Lauren. Like I said, she's a person. You don't pay for people. At least—*I don't*.

Instead, I had other plans.

Earlier, when Vance had pulled the security camera footage onto the living room TV, I saw Lauren—and two other people that I was gonna have to kill.

Even in the best of circumstances, even if these two men were the kindest kidnappers in the game—I couldn't just buy her off them. If that were the case, they'd get their money, but Silas would never get her. And soon they would begin to wonder why Silas was still after a girl that they, by all accounts, had already sold to him. I could never be that sloppy.

From the moment I opened the door, I knew that I was looking at two dead bodies. I knew I was going to kill them.

I had to. I didn't really have much of a choice.

However, after seeing the way they'd manhandled her, after seeing her tear-stained cheeks, after seeing her cuts and bruises, and after hearing the words, '*I swear I won't let Grip touch you again.*'—I didn't just *have* to kill them.

I wanted to.

Chapter Three

KAIN

"We party like rock stars, we sex like porn stars, I'll take you a million bars..."

Cierra's taste in music, unsurprisingly, was trash.

The house was full of strangers. *"Just some friends from school,"* my older sister had promised, before I'd agreed to let her have her birthday party here, at the house. As per usual, Silas was out of town on business, so the only person she had to convince was me.

I should have said no.

'Just some friends from school,' actually turned out to be *everybody* from school. There were people in here who didn't even know who this party was for. But they were all too happy to touch shit they couldn't afford to break, and lap up as much free alcohol as they could handle. I turned down the air conditioning four more degrees. *All this fuckin' body heat...*

Against the backdrop of *yet another* Trina song, I heard something glass shatter in the kitchen.

Do you even wanna look?

Drawing in a long, calming breath, I went to inspect the source of the sound. A group of people had gathered around at least half a dozen shattered wine glasses, picking the shards up from the ground. I made a mental note to remind myself to buy wine glasses this weekend. As for right now, as long as Cierra's drunk guests still had enough sense to clean up after themselves—*fuck it*...

I needed to loosen up. It was a party.

It was a really shitty party—filled with aggravating strangers, and bad music, but it was a party. I opened up the fridge to see what kind of drinks Cierra had stocked for her birthday.

White spirits.

Not a single bottle of anything brown.

Nice, I thought sarcastically. Cierra's taste in alcohol is trash, too, I realized, reaching for a bottle of *Absolut Elyx*, and then grabbing a shot glass. For a buzz, I could do four. I wasn't trying to get drunk. I was just trying to relax.

The glass was halfway to my face when a hand came up and snatched it out of mine. *You have got to be fucking kidding me*...

"I know, I know," the girl cooed at my expression, her eyes apologizing as if she had no choice but to do what she'd just done. "But I *really* need this shot."

She sipped at it.

I didn't think I'd seen someone sip straight vodka since high school. *Is she… Is she doing this for the first time?*

"Ugh, this is terrible," she grumbled between chugs. *Yep*. I let out a short, inaudible laugh. *Unbelievable*. I had every reason to be irritated, but I was just…amused. "People drink that for fun?" she asked no one in particular after she'd finished. "I could barely get that down."

"That's why they usually just toss it back," I replied, surprising her—and myself.

Her eyebrows came together skeptically. "Like… all in one go?" she asked.

I certainly didn't imagine I'd be spending my Friday night explaining the logistics of taking shots to a girl who couldn't have been a day under eighteen. *Shouldn't she know this by now?*

It was then that I got a look at what she had on. Her red dress, although kind of working for her, was so out of place. She was dressed like she was getting ready to tell me about all the great things God has done in her life.

My head tilted to the side, confused at first. *Is she in the wrong house?*

"Okay, I'm ready for my second try," she announced, shaking the glass expectantly as though I was some bartender. It would have been very like me to simply leave the bottle on the counter and tell her to pour her own shot, but one look at her dark eyes—shining with an almost child-like naïveté—and I was suddenly unsure of myself. In a place like this, with eyes like that, she could get herself into a lot of trouble.

It wasn't like me to give a shit, to be honest.

And yet...

I poured the second shot, letting the alcohol flow just shy of the glass's rim. Her eyes grew to the size of quarters upon realizing how much she had to throw back. Despite myself, I cracked a smile. She was kinda cute.

"Ugh, that burns," she told me after tossing it all down, shaking her shoulders as if to get the alcohol's warming effect out of her system.

I grimaced at her little dance, my eyes going above her head to Amir coming up behind her. Trying to talk over the music, my friend was shouting when he spoke.

"Yo, you know where Cici is?"

Of course.

Nevermind that I'd literally just arrived in Miami from Tally only four hours ago. Nevermind that I hadn't seen the nigga since New Year's. With him, it was Cierra all day, every day. I could just tell by observing Amir's whack ass that being in love wasn't for me.

"She's around here somewhere," I shrugged, my eyes glancing down at Red Dress absently, as if a small part of me was worried about her walking off.

Evidently, she was really good at minding her own business, choosing to occupy herself with her phone rather than eavesdrop on my conversation with Amir. She didn't even bother turning around to see who I was talking to. *Interesting*, I noted, at the same time also noticing she'd yet to walk away.

Amir followed my gaze, his eyes falling on the back of her head.

'*That's you?*' he mouthed, pointing at her as his eyes traveled down her backside. '*Damn*,' I read his lips say once his eyes fell to her ass.

Something about the gesture didn't sit quite well with me. I tried to rationalize it by telling myself it was because Amir was in a whole ass relationship with my sister, but—come on. Their relationship was *their* relationship. It had never been like me to concern myself with what my sister and my best friend had going on. That momentary spike in my blood pressure over Amir looking at Red Dress' ass—that was for something else entirely.

"Go find your girl," I said with a nod of my head, tone subtly impatient.

When I turned my attention back to Red Dress, she, of course, had her glass out for another drink. "I don't feel anything yet," she explained.

Last one, I told myself, giving her what she asked for. She tossed that one back like it was water, saying something about how she couldn't taste it anymore. Her eyes darted across the room, and I watched as her front teeth sunk into her lower lip anxiously. She watched the other party guests with an almost longing look. As if she craved a sense of belonging.

I shook my head, trying to snap myself out of whatever it was that had me staring so fucking hard.

Catching me off guard, she snapped her head back in my direction and slammed the glass on the counter, practically demanding a fourth shot. *A'ight, ma, you gettin' a lil too comfortable*.

I thought it.

But I didn't say it.

Oddly, all I did was look at her, my eyes scanning her delicate features analytically. Although four shots weren't nearly enough to get me sauced, it was certainly enough for me to get slightly buzzed. I could only imagine the effect it'd have on a woman her height and weight.

Her eyebrows came up expectantly, an impatience in them. It seemed like she was holding her own pretty well for a first-timer. So it didn't seem like an all-the-way bad idea as I poured her another. This time, however, I gave her a little less than I'd been giving her for the first three.

She stared at the glass after it was filled, her eyes beginning to get a dreamlike quality to them.

"My sister is such a bitch," she disclosed randomly, tossing her organized curls back as she tilted backward for her fourth drink. "She's the selfishest person I know."

Her speech was a little slurred.

Ah, fuck. I regretted that last shot. She had about fifteen minutes before all those drinks hit her at once, and if she was already slurring... *Fuck.*

"Most selfish," she corrected her grammar, seemingly trying to hold onto her sobriety. Her eyes rose from her glass, looking up at me with something that resembled embarrassment. Her eyes were dark brown, as was her skin—a perfect clarity in both. I caught myself not blinking. *Damn, she's really pretty.*

I blinked away the thought just as she rose her glass again, asking for a fifth.

Sizing her, I drew the bottle back. *Absolutely not.*

Her eyebrows shot up. "No, you don't understand."

With her hand, she beckoned me to come in closer. When I didn't budge, she only got more aggressive, shooting me an eager, dimpled smile. Something in my chest jumped—and I *promptly* ignored it. Playing it off, I gave in to her persuasion, leaning down to hear what was so important.

She cupped her hand around my ear and whispered, "I'm not drunk."

Well, I hadn't thought so until now.

Releasing a sigh, I started to put some distance between her and I. A sound like a whimper came out of her and she reached out to grab the front of my shirt. "No, stop. I'm not finished," she whined.

My eyes dropped to her hand, which had my shirt balled within a fist. My first reaction was to be confused. Because of my last name, people had their assumptions about what I was like, and treated me accordingly. The sheer weirdness of her behavior threw me off. Strangers rarely invaded my personal space like this.

She's drunk, I reminded myself.

As if reading my mind, she said, "I swear I'm not drunk. Not yet. I need another drink. Fuck being sober. Fuck my sister Morgan." She stopped to clear her throat, and shouted louder, "Fuck Morgan!"

What the hell...

After prying away her tight grip on my shirt, I finally spoke.

"Ain't you think you've had enough?"

Stunned, her eyebrows rose at my imposing tone, and her posture straightened. I watched as she took a moment to collect herself before her eyes shot back to me and the brightest smile stretched across her face, trying to play off her initial reaction. *Those fucking dimples again*. There was another jump in my chest.

Shit—what is wrong with me?

"Could I just have one more?" she complained, her voice drunkenly childish. When I didn't react, she batted her eyelashes, raised her glass, and giggled. "I swear I'm not drunk."

Yes, the hell you are.

I got this sneaking feeling that she would only keep asking, and I didn't know how many no's I had left in me if she continued to look at me like that. With a shake of my head, I backed away from her, creating some distance until I ultimately ran back into Amir.

"Yooo." I stopped him before he could walk off. "Take this bottle. And if that girl—" I gestured to Red Dress, not really checking if she was looking "—asks you for anythin' to drink, could you make sure you get her some water?"

Amir grimaced at the weird request but didn't comment on it, taking the vodka off my hands.

"*Absolut Elyx*," he read off the feminine bottle, an amused smile forming. Of course, he went in on me for it. "Does drinking this make you feel like a bad bitch?"

"Man, shut up," I laughed.

For that entire evening, I was distracted. Against a sea of denim and neutral colors, her cherry red dress kept popping into my peripheral vision. One minute, she was in the kitchen, looking for somewhere to stuff her purse, the next she was in the living room, letting loose to the beat of the music. For a while, I was all too aware of her presence.

And then I wasn't.

I was in the middle of a conversation I was half listening to, when I caught myself actually looking for signs of her. As I felt a headache coming on, the fact that she was nowhere to be seen only served to make this party even less interesting. My conversation partner was in the middle of her sentence when I excused myself, headed in the direction of my room.

Cierra's party could continue just fine without me.

The door to my bedroom was closed.

A party with well over seventy young people was going on. Someone was bound to come upstairs looking for someplace to fuck. My room, however, was off limits.

The room was dark as I stepped in, but the sounds of shuffling definitely gave away the presence of unwelcome intruders. Forgoing the light switch, I simply moved deeper into the space, getting closer to the natural moonlight that streamed in from an open window.

"Get out of my room." The anger in my voice was tired. I was done with tonight before it even started. "Y'all are gonna have to find someplace else to fuck." I raised a hand to block the view of the nigga getting dressed in front of me. "As in, outta this house."

Noting that his girl was seriously taking her time, I tossed a pressing look her way.

The dress was what I saw first.

Unzipped and drooping off her shoulder, pulled high up her thighs, disheveled. The confusion in my eyes dissipated as I eventually made sense of the situation.

"What the hell…"

Rape.

"*Yooo*, what the *fuck* is this?" I was livid. A surprising reaction.

Because I knew stuff like this happened at house parties all the time. There are full-fledged courses out there dedicated to teaching niggas to not touch what they shouldn't. It still *happens*. All the time, actually, which is the fucked up part. Though, within this context, it was even more fucked up. After pumping her full of shots, I couldn't help but feel partially responsible. A pang of guilt shot through my chest.

The rapist acted as though he couldn't hear me, shakily stringing his belt through his pants.

Surprisingly, my vision went red then, my head hot with a flaming rage.

"Answer me when I'm talkin' to you!" My arm came up, slamming into his chest and forcing him against the wall. The back of his head crashed into it, giving off an audible cracking sound. I couldn't be sure if that was the drywall, or if it was his skull. I didn't give a shit. "What *the fuck* are you doing?"

* * *

The first night I met Lauren Caplan, I was in the right place at the right time.

She was a bright-eyed nineteen-year-old girl, going through the motions of her first ever college house party, and she'd fallen prey to someone who was all too happy to take advantage of her. Had I been just a few minutes delayed, her life would have changed forever that night. Oftentimes I think about it, and I feel a sense of relief.

I stopped it.

I wasn't too late.

I saved her.

I saved that light in her eyes.

The light in her eyes was gone now. For me, that was harder to look at than the bruises. Jerome's words echoed in my head as I lead him and his partner further into the house.

I swear I won't let Grip touch you again.

Whatever happened—I *didn't* stop it, I *was* too late, I *didn't* save her. And now the joyful glitter in her eyes was gone like it never existed. *This week just keeps getting worse*.

"We got company," I informed Vance as Lauren and the two strangers followed in behind me.

There must've been something off about my energy because Vance squinted as though he was having trouble recognizing me before replying, "I can see that."

"Yeah, we finally bagged Miami's Most Wanted," Jerome informed behind me as if expecting to be congratulated for it. Vance only blinked, setting the remote in his hand down on the coffee table before throwing me a questioning look.

"Remember the girl I was telling you about the other day?" I posed, explaining, "This is her."

Vance raised a single eyebrow, confusion still weighing heavy on his features.

In the days that came after Memphis, I'd been spending a lot of time at home. Depression ate away at my better judgement one particular evening, and in a Hennessy-induced confessional, I confided in Vance.

I told him about Lauren.

Nothing too deep, just that she was from a different world, and that we would probably never work out in the grand scheme of things. To my wonder, he seemed to be completely unsurprised by my confession— as though my eventual falling in love with someone I had no business falling for was the predictable outcome.

Falling in love…

I didn't say that; Vance did. Although, I couldn't recall disagreeing.

What I'd neglected to mention was that Lauren wasn't just any girl. She was the daughter of Miami's state attorney—the prosecutor in my father's case. I'd skipped that in my recap because it added a layer of questioning that I wasn't ready to debate. Even though I trusted Lauren with my life lately, in everyone else's eyes, my relationship created weak spots in the impenetrable world of my family. I understood both sides, which made it impossible to argue.

To them, Lauren was an outsider—the worst kind of outsider, at that. And they weren't wrong.

To me, however, being with Lauren was like laying your head down on a pillow after days of sleep deprivation. It was a symbolic analogy at first, until I realized that being with Lauren really did make me sleep easier. For a while, she was the one thing in my life that didn't add to the noise; she was my peace.

Vance offered Lauren a seat on the sectional, saying something about how she looked spent. Lauren eyed the unfamiliar face warily, casting a questioning look my way.

"Go," I encouraged.

I couldn't have her so close by my side with the plan that was formulating in my head. Ideally, it would have been best if she wasn't in the room at all.

The first night I met Lauren, when I happened upon her as a disheveled mess, an unwilling participant trapped between my bed and a rapist—I was fully prepared to commit the most unforgivable sin. Why? Because he deserved it. Because she was helpless. Because I was pissed the fuck off.

I couldn't remember the last time anger had consumed me so powerfully. Anger that boiled red and hot, vibrating every cell in my body. The kind of anger that makes your hands itch for the feeling of a dying pulse.

And then she closed her eyes. She shut them so tight, crinkles formed at the bridge of her nose. Some people get attacked and they want to see their offenders burned at the stake. Lauren, however, couldn't even stomach his distress. Miraculously, I found myself cooling off at the sight of her, somehow coming down from an anger that was so strong that it initially felt permanent.

I'd breathed out a sigh of resignation and lowered the gun. Nobody died that night. She didn't need to see that, especially not in the emotional headspace she was in. Instead, I stayed by her side, watched her sleep for hours, and when she woke up... I fell for her—*hard*.

"How'd she get that bruise on her cheek?" My tone was casual even though I was furious. In my peripheral vision, I could see Lauren curiously brushing her fingers along the discoloration, being made aware it was there for the first time. The second she touched it, she drew back and snatched her hand away, wincing.

"You want some ice for that, ma?" Vance asked her quietly, to which she shook her head.

Jerome's eyebrows came together skeptically, confusion etched into his expression over her being treated like some sort of esteemed guest. That should've been his first sign that something wasn't right. However, he didn't outwardly question it so much as awkwardly grimace at the spectacle.

"Her face," I brought it back up, tone still easy as I ambled over closer to the two men standing off the side of my living room. For a brief moment, I looked at the white carpet beneath my feet and inwardly groaned.

Blood is a bitch to get out of white carpet. "What happened?"

An unusual cross between a squint and a sheepish smile spread across Jerome's face as he tossed a look to his partner. Something was apparently funny. The joke was clearly lost on me. "You wanna tell them what happened to her face, Grip?"

Grip fixed his eyes to look at her, and he said the words, "Lil mama's feisty." That same anger I felt the night Lauren and I first met began to make my hands hot. "I'm sure Silas don't mind that I put her in her place a little."

I made a mental note to make sure that one would die painfully and slow. When I looked back at Lauren, I expected tears. Instead, she was surprisingly together, her chin resting on a raised hand...almost *boredly*.

Strange.

Although I certainly wasn't disappointed that Lauren seemed to be handling things with visible ease, it just wasn't the comportment I was expecting. Lauren—I'd come to accept—was a crier. She cried when she was sad, when she was scared, when she was happy, for just about everything. My girl cried enough for the both of us.

However, not now.

"So the money," Jerome reminded, dragging his sneakers along the white carpet; a move that would've irritated me if I hadn't already decided I was about to create a bigger mess. My eyes briefly fell to the dent protruding out from Jerome's waist, where he'd patted for his gun not too long ago, when he felt threatened.

Cowards are always trying to let people know they're armed. Because guns are supposed to scare people. Guns protect because they're supposed to make potential attackers think twice about trying you. *Don't touch that man, he'll shoot you*, I'm supposed to think.

Not exactly.

"Yeah, the money," I nodded, stepping forward. Except, I wasn't trying to get closer to Jerome. I was trying to get closer to his gun. "One question, though."

"What is it?" he asked as I took another step.

"Are you left-handed or right?"

"Uh…" His eyebrows came together questioningly at the seemingly random question. *What does this have to do with my money*, he seemed to be thinking. "I'm right-handed."

"Thanks."

Before it could register, I went for his right-side arm, twisting it behind him tightly. Left with his non-dominant hand, Jerome simply wasn't fast enough for his weapon. It was already in my possession.

When I was thirteen, my father taught me to never reach for my weapon until I was ready to shoot somebody. The quickest way to make sure you get killed with your own gun is to let someone desperate know you have one before you're ready to use it. If it's life or death—people take risks, and soon your gun starts to look like a way out.

With Jerome's gun in my hand, I now understood exactly what Silas was talking about.

"Yo, what the *fuck*." Jerome struggled to shake himself loose.

Ignoring him, my eyes darted to his partner, Grip, who stood more confused than surprised. Neither of them had fully caught on yet.

"You got a gun on you?" Before he could lie to me, I amended, "Lift up your shirt and turn around."

Grip started to ask, "What is—"

I fired a shot into the back of Jerome's knee. He buckled, swearing loudly as I let go of his arm.

"That wasn't a request," I clarified, watching the red spread onto the clean carpet.

As his partner writhed in excruciating pain, Grip's eyes grew larger than I thought possible. For a moment of confusion, Grip went into a brief state of shock, before he quickly gathered his wits and started to beg.

"I left my gun in the car! I left my gun in the car!" he shouted twice, his words sounding like a plea as he lifted his shirt to prove it. "See?"

I tossed a look back to a cursing Jerome, who was holding the leaking wound at his knee. He was making an awful lot of noise. When I raised the barrel to his forehead, he'd barely gotten a word out before I blasted us all into absolute silence. My hand came up to wipe the residual splatter off my face.

It wasn't quiet for long.

As the sudden death of his partner fully hit, Grip started yelling.

"Yo! *Yooooo!* I don't want it! I don't need the money, man. What the fuck! WHAT THE FUCK!"

Pushing out a breath, I swallowed down the rising gag in my throat. *Fuck, I hate the smell of blood.*

"Could you just…" I raised my free hand to pinch the skin between my eyes as I closed them. Gunshots make my ears ring. Grip's screaming was making it worse. "…be *quiet* for a second."

And he shut right up.

I might've found that funny if I wasn't so aware of Lauren's presence in this room, a spectator to all of this—seeing the parts of me I tried to hide from her for so long. Needing to keep my momentum, I didn't dare look at her. Instead, I drew in steady breaths, waiting for the incessant ringing in my ears to pass.

As my hearing normalized, I started to take apart the gun, pulling out the magazine and letting all of the remaining bullets fall onto the carpet beside Jerome's lifeless body. When I cut my eyes back to Grip, his shoulders had slumped, relaxing, mistaking my actions as a promise of mercy.

Nah.

I had something special for his ass.

And all I needed for it were my God-given hands.

Raising two fingers, I beckoned Grip to come closer. He hesitated at first, but ultimately decided it would be better he come to me than make me come to him.

In truth, it made no difference at all.

"So she was feisty, huh?" I reiterated with a tilt of my head. It was only now that he seemed to realize this wasn't about money at all. His hands came up in premature surrender.

"Look, I didn't—" He lost some of his nerve as I stepped closer, getting in his face. "I didn't touch her."

Lie.

The bruise on my girl's cheek said different.

My knuckles slammed into the side of his face, giving off an audible crunching sound. First lick in, I let out a relaxing sigh and cracked my neck to loosen up. After a week of bullshit, kicking this nigga's ass was about to be damn near therapeutic.

"Man, I swear!" he shouted, tossing up his fists to block any more oncoming blows. His eyes cut to Lauren's direction behind me. "Tell him!"

Grabbing at the back of his head, I smashed my knee into his nose before I calmly expressed, "Don't talk to her."

"I tried!" he confessed holding onto his bleeding nostrils. "I t-tried and sh-she *threatened* me. I backed off."

That doesn't even sound like Lauren.

"Okay," was all I said to that. I was done talking. I punched him again, and again, and again.

Until I lost count.

Until my fingers felt numb.

Until my hands were wet and colored red.

Until he stopped making sounds.

Until, with the last blow, a deafening snap echoed, and his neck twisted unnaturally.

And he stopped breathing.

When I finally rose to my feet, ready to face the reactions of the other two people in the room, I was not surprised to find that Lauren was covering her ears, eyes shut so tight that her skin crinkled at her nose bridge.

Vance, however, stood there, eyes open and nearly speechless.

My uncle looked at my bloodied hands for a stretched second before dragging his gaze back up to my eyes. When he finally did speak, he said the most insulting thing he could think of in that moment.

"You really are your father's son."

Chapter Four

KAIN

The water streaming off my hands ran red into the drain, and then pink, and then clear.

I was at the kitchen sink, washing off the blood on my hands, two bodies soiling the living room carpet behind me. The two most important people in my life looked on, neither of them saying anything as I pulled my phone from my back pocket.

"I know it's late," I said into the receiver once he picked up on the other end. It was almost two o'clock in the morning, and my friend Marlon had definitely been asleep. "I made a bit of a mess…"

"What kind of mess?" he asked, and I could hear him getting out of bed.

"The only kind of mess I'd be callin' at two AM over."

"How many?"

"Two."

"Why?"

"She got picked up," I replied simply.

This put a little more energy behind his words.

"Wait, *huh*? You mean Lauren?" Marlon had a bit of a soft spot for my girlfriend. Not the kind of soft spot that made me look at him crazy, of course. It was protective, which I had no problem with. My guess was that Lauren reminded him of his younger sister, Eden. They both had that doe-eyed innocence about them—the kind of energy you just felt compelled to protect. "Is she a'ight?"

I glanced in her direction, and in trying to describe her, the description that immediately came to mind was *tired*. Nothing more, nothing less.

"For the most part," I answered Marlon's question.

"I'm on my way."

Saturday, March 12ᵗʰ, 2016
(Fourteen Weeks Ago)

Lauren had just pulled out of Marlon's driveway when I walked back into the house.

I half expected to be bombarded with questions by my friends, harassed for an explanation. Instead, the only person I found waiting for me when I stepped inside was Amir, lounging around in Marlon's living room, a freshly rolled dutch between his fingers. Knowing what was coming, I took a seat across.

"You ever hear of hero syndrome?" Amir asked before taking a long drag at the blunt in his hand. Confused, my eyebrows came together questioningly, as he spread the weed smell throughout.

"I think you just made that up."

He made a face, and clarified. "You know what I mean... Savior complexes... Superman Syndrome... Captain Save-a-Hoe headass."

I could see where this was going. "It ain't even like that."

"So enlighten me." He stretched out an arm and welcomed an explanation. "You wanna tell me why all this time and energy is going into a bitch who—"

"Mind your fuckin' mouth."

"You see!?" Amir set the blunt down and slouched, resting his elbows on his knees as he said, "That's the shit I'm talking about! Since when do you give a fuck about who I call a bitch and who I—"

"I really couldn't care less, Am. But what you won't do is talk that shit in front of me. You know her name. Use it."

"Hmm," he pondered before shaking his head. "You playin' games, bruh. I know you go for them regular girls, 'cause you like to trick yourself into thinkin' you normal. But lemme make this fuckin' clear before you get yourself in some serious mess—you ain't *fuckin'* normal, Kain. You ain't never gonna be normal."

When I didn't say anything, he continued.

"And she ain't normal either. Lauren ain't your usual brand of outsider. Her father—"

"Man, I know."

"Do you though?"

"What am I supposed to do? Leave her defenseless? If Silas ever gets her—if he doesn't kill her immediately, he's gonna make her wish he did."

"Okay, and?" Amir shrugged, not seeing the problem.

"I can't let that happen to her."

"Who died, and made it your job to start savin' people?" Amir argued, frustration thick in his voice. "Bringing me back to my original point—hero syndrome."

"Not people," I corrected. "Just her."

"Sounds like a lot of fuss over a girl who—"

"If you don't want to help me out with this, then don't, Amir."

"Oh, I *don't* want to," he made clear. "Just like Marlon and Jay probably don't really want to, either. But we all see the writing on the wall. Girls like that... they *talk* under pressure. If we let Silas get her now, the first thing she gon' do when she feels her life is at stake, is speak *your* name. You too fuckin' pussy-whipped to see that. We ain't protectin' her for these next six weeks, Kain. We protectin' *you*."

"Nah, I'm doing it 'cause I like her." My head twisted in the direction of Marlon's voice leaning into the threshold that connected the living room and his bedroom. "Kain is grown. I could give a shit about what he's gettin' himself into. His girl, though... You ain't never lived with Silas, Amir, so you just don't know."

"The fuck's that supposed to mean?" Amir retorted.

Marlon and I went way back.

When I was four years old, Silas got a girlfriend named Marie, and she was a stunner. So much so that Silas didn't even seem to care that she had three kids of her own. She was his main woman for at least ten years, keeping her kids in tow. I grew up with Marlon and his younger siblings, and over time, all three of them started to feel like my siblings, too.

Living at the big house with Silas gave Marlon the exact same insight that I had. Unlike my other two friends, he knew precisely what Lauren was up against.

"What I'm sayin' is," Marlon started, ambling over and picking up the blunt Amir had set down. He took a drag before shaking his head and blowing out a cloud around his head. "Silas won't kill that girl. Her father's a state's attorney. Silas will keep her as a pet, and hold her captive under the most disgusting level of torture you can imagine. He'll taunt her father with hints about her whereabouts and condition. Not enough to incriminate himself, but just enough so that her father knows he has her. He'll have her father thinking that if he loses the case, his daughter can come home. He might even lull *her* into a false sense of hope with that shit, too. And when he no longer needs her..." Marlon took another puff before finishing his sentence "...*then* he'll kill her. So I'm not doing this for Kain at all. I'm doing it for her. Because nobody deserves that shit."

From the kitchen, Jay called, "I like the sound of that. Yeah. You can protect Kain all you want, Amir, *witcho gay ass*! It's the girl I'm protecting."

Whatever their motivations, I was just relieved to have all three of my friends on board.

"Hey, Button," Marlon greeted Lauren, concerned apprehension thick in his tone. A few months ago, some dude had grabbed Lauren as she was having lunch on campus. Marlon intercepted just before she could be forced into a car, and since then, he'd been calling her Panic Button—or just Button for short. "What happened to your face?"

I tried to listen in for her response, but I couldn't hear it, as I dragged the bodies off the living room carpet and onto the wood flooring of the kitchen. Without my asking, Vance handed me a canister of *Resolve* carpet cleaner wordlessly. Before I covered the blood stains with the stain-lifting powder, I doused the mess in ice water.

Years of watching blood stains get removed from various surfaces had my movements downright automated. I knew the steps in my sleep. Ice cold water, never hot. *Resolve* powder sits on top for at least twelve hours, or until it dries. Vacuum, and then bleach.

"You mind tellin' me what the fuck is happening?" Vance whispered harshly to the side of my face.

Not responding right away, I shook the last of the powder onto the dirtied parts of the carpet, removing all signs of any red. I sighed before I started to explain.

"My girlfriend—the one I told you about—just so happens to be the daughter of the state attorney for the Miami-Dade County district, the prosecutor on Dad's trial this August. Dad has a bounty out for her, and I've been blocking it for about three months now." My explanation was concise, straight to the point. No room for conversation. "Now if you'll excuse me, I gotta go burn my clothes."

Vance grabbed at my shoulder, his grip tight and confrontational. My eyes fell to his hand, and I reminded myself that this was my uncle. However aggressive the invasion of space, now was really not the time to start another fight.

"Whatever you're about to say—I know," I informed tiredly, keeping my voice low so that only he could hear me. "But that's my girl over there, so I don't care."

"You don't think you're a little in over your head, Youngblood?" Vance questioned. I shrugged his hand off my shoulder.

"Nah." I looked around the room, acknowledging the mostly cleaned up mess. "I got this."

Before going up the stairs, I asked something of my friend.

"Marlon, could you get her out of here. My house in Pembroke Pines is not too far." Lauren had been in the room with these dead bodies for entirely way too long. Marlon turned his head to look at her as if to say, *I'm ready when you are*.

Lauren's gaze darted from me to my friend rapidly, and I didn't just see the anxiety flash in her dark eyes. I think I somehow felt it, too.

"You'd rather stay here," I gathered.

"I... I don't want to be by myself." Lauren wrapped her arms around herself, something she always did whenever she felt less than secure. I didn't bother with pointing out to her that she wouldn't be alone, but with Marlon. I understood, without her saying so, that if I wasn't there, she might as well be by herself.

Alright. Maybe Vance was right. I might've been in over my head.

"I'll move the bodies." Vance broke the silence while I tried to think, his offer taking me by surprise. "You seem like you'd be sloppy with it anyways. Better I do it."

"I got the car." Marlon offered to get rid of the car they'd arrived in. "I'll take it to that shop on Biscayne to get pulled apart first thing in the morning."

"Don't burn your clothes until the sun is out," Vance advised. "It's two o'clock in the goddamn morning. Backyard fires at this time of night—that's suspicious, kid."

Sighing, I returned my attention to Lauren, nodding for her to follow me up the stairs. I hadn't realized how much I was dreading the last thing on my to-do list until it became the only thing left to do.

I had to talk to her.

* * *

The first thing she did once we were alone, was apologize.

I wouldn't let her, raising a hand in a silent plea to get her to stop. I hated it when Lauren apologized for things that weren't her fault. My eyes regretfully passed over the cuts and bruises that blemished her once perfect brown skin.

"Don't apologize for anything. Just follow me into the bathroom right quick."

Lauren didn't question it. Instead, she wordlessly stepped through the threshold as soon as I opened the door, passing through my closet before stopping at the bathroom sink and turning to face me.

To the question in her eyes, I quietly instructed for her to, "Hop onto the counter for me."

And she did, leveling out our heights so that we'd be eye-to-eye. With her seated, I crouched down to the cabinets under the sink, rummaging around until I found what I was looking for. My bathroom was kept stocked like a hotel thanks to Silas' diligent housekeeping staff. I'd never really appreciated the over-the-top nature of the makeshift pharmacy under my sink until now.

In the empty space beside Lauren's lap, I set the first-aid kit down onto the counter. Neither of us spoke as I examined the damage done, gently turning her head so that I could get a better look at the darkening bruise spreading just below her left eye. The skin at the lesion had thinned over the swelling, not quite bleeding, but not quite dry either.

"So," I started, pulling an antiseptic wipe from the box of supplies. "Let's start from the beginning."

I was ripping the package open when she pushed out a breath and shook her head. "I didn't mean to get myself in this situ—"

"Hey," I cut her off, raising an eyebrow. "That sounds like an apology. Just tell me what happened."

"Well—*ouch*! That stings!" She snatched her head back and away from the alcohol wipe, her eyebrows coming together in outrage. In spite of myself, I cracked a half-smile.

"It's necessary," I responded, guiding the napkin back to her cheek. "Talk to me."

"My dad kicked me out."

"In the middle of the night?"

She nodded. *Goddamn, Joshua Caplan really ain't shit.* "My mom tried to get me to stay, but I don't know... Once I heard the words out of his mouth..."

"...It didn't feel right to stay," I finished her sentence.

"Me and my pride," she muttered, scolding herself for her choice. Maybe she thought she was beating me to the punch. Personally, I had no desire to criticize her for her decision.

I tossed the wet wipe in the trash; it had turned from white to pink.

"And then what happened?" I asked as I uncapped a tube of *Neosporin*. I tried to keep my touch light as I applied the pain relieving ointment to her cheek.

"I walked to a bus station."

"The one just outside of Coconut Grove?" I asked, reaching for some gauze and a large *Band-Aid*. "That's at least six miles out from where you stay."

"Yeah." She nodded. "I know. I ran the first four."

"Sounds like you wore yourself out." Over the gauze pad, I gently adhered the waterproof *Band-Aid* to cover up the entire wound. Now that I didn't have to see it anymore, I felt a little better myself. "Were you planning on goin' somewhere?"

"No, I just needed to sit down."

"Stick out your arm for me," I instructed, pulling loose another alcohol wipe. "And so the bus station is where you got picked up?"

"Not far from it." She drew in a sharp breath through her teeth, as the alcohol seeped into her less serious cuts. "After I shot this guy named Swiss, the other two pulled up and—"

"After you did what?"

"*Yeahhhh*," she said the word slowly, her voice regretful. "I shot someone."

I didn't say anything. I might've been speechless.

"He didn't die. I closed my eyes. It hit his arm. Lucky shot." *That's an unlucky shot where I come from.* "I dropped the gun after the first shot."

"Too loud?"

She nodded. "So loud that it hurt. After that—me against three. Some things you just can't prepare for... They dropped the one I injured off at the hospital—"

"Sounds like a loose end." The thought of having to hunt down this unforeseen third person was already making me tired.

Lauren shook her head. "I really don't think you have to worry about him. The other two were going to double cross him anyway. They were going to take the money they got for me and cut him out of the separation. When he can't get a hold of them, he'll probably just think they hightailed it to Mexico, or something, without him."

"You're handling all this a lot better than I anticipated," I finally addressed the elephant in the room.

"I'm strong," she assured, not sounding all the way assertive. More convincingly, she revised, "Well… I'm *stronger*."

"Did anything else happen tonight that you wanna tell me about?" My fingers brushed over the scratches on her skin regretfully. *This wouldn't have happened if I sought her out after Memphis*, I found myself thinking.

"I wasn't raped, if that's what you're alluding to," she stated rather bluntly. "Grip, the one that you *um*…" She put up her fists and did a *really* bad one-two combo, indicating she was talking about the second one I killed. "…he punched me, and tried to get me to go down on him. And uh… I told him I'd bite it off."

That was objectively funny, but because it was Lauren, I couldn't even crack a smile. I was too angry.

"Did you really?" I encouraged her to keep talking as I pressed a smaller waterproof *Band-Aid* onto one of her elbows.

"It's not as brave as it sounds," she confessed with a casual shrug. "I knew they couldn't kill me."

Something was off.

"Do you think you might be dissociating right now?" I asked bluntly.

"Oooh," she cooed, impressed. "Bringing out the psychology terminology, are we?"

"You're avoiding the question," I informed. "It's okay, Lauren. Coping mechanisms are for coping. They're normal."

She met my eyes directly. "I'm not coping."

"You just watched me kill two niggas in my living room. And, to add insult to injury, you shot someone for the first time tonight." I tilted my head to the side skeptically. "You almost seem...*normal*. Happy, even. Something ain't right."

"I'm not happy." Lauren closed her eyes and drew in a calming inhale. "I'm relieved," she breathed out.

I nodded, thinking I understood. "You thought you were going to die tonight," I assumed.

"No, it's not that," she replied. I raised an eyebrow and she finally opened her eyes to look at me. They were glossy and turning pink at the corners. "Seventy-three people, Kain. I thought *you* died."

Oh.

"Seventy-three people," she repeated. "And I... I couldn't know for sure if you..." When her head slumped forward and her forehead landed on my shoulder, I knew it was because she didn't want me to see her tears. "But now... Now I know."

Chapter Five

KAIN

I wasn't sleeping.

For the first time in six days, however, it was a choice. Tonight, I chose to lie awake and watch her sleep, focusing on the tranquility of her breathing. There was beauty in her vulnerability, in the unspoken declaration of trust with her ability to fall asleep in this house—the most dangerous place for her to be.

A sound like a whine came out of her unexpectedly, and she stirred uncomfortably. Her hands stretched out, feeling for me before finally settling on my chest. Calming down, her breathing slowed and she inched in closer, allowing her forehead to sink into the fabric of my shirt.

"Was that a nightmare?" I checked to see if she was awake.

No more than four hours ago, she'd watched me kill two people without hesitation. Nightmares were to be expected. If I was being completely honest with myself, the opportunity to watch Lauren sleep wasn't the only thing keeping me awake. I wasn't ready for whatever my subconscious mind was cooking up for me in my dreams.

And so I stayed awake.

"I'm okay," she replied tiredly against my shirt, taking me by surprise. Her voice was still unconvincing when she repeated, "I'm okay."

A nightmare for sure.

"Go back to sleep, Lauren." My arm wrapped around her protectively, holding her against the steady beating of my heart. "I'm here. I've got you."

Lauren shook herself loose from my embrace, creating some distance so that she could get a look at me. In the dawn's dim lighting, I could only just make out her face.

"Kain," she said my name with caution. Just a slight deviation from her usual tone, and she could send my pulse racing with anxiety. I hated that so much. "About that night..."

Ah, fuck...

"Lauren, I don't want to talk about that night."

"Even—"

"Whatever you're about to say—yes. Even that. I don't want to talk about it."

"But..."

I think I was more so begging, instead of asking, when I said, "Please."

Lauren, it seemed, simply couldn't help it. Her voice was sympathetic when she whispered, "You have to talk about it."

"Not with you," I hit back, knowing it would hurt her feelings. But it was true. Lauren was the last person I wanted to talk about this with.

Amir always used to say that messing around with her was gonna get me killed. Ironically, messing around with Lauren saved my fucking life.

And every time I looked at her, a little part of me was all too aware that she was the reason I was here, and Amir was dead. Of course I didn't blame her for Amir's death (that was all on me), but it was impossible to not acknowledge what happened. Amir was only at *Poseidon* that night because I would've rather been with her.

It was supposed to be me.

But I knew I couldn't tell Lauren that. Lauren loved me, and because she loved me, she would never see the reality of Amir dying in my place as a bad thing. And I just… I couldn't talk to her about his death, knowing full well that deep down some part of her was grateful for the outcome. Facing that would just piss me off.

The silence of the room was uncomfortable now. Lauren lied awake, eyes wide open, but, heeding my request, she was no longer talking.

I couldn't be sure what I wanted anymore.

I didn't want Lauren to talk about that night, but feeling like I'd silenced her didn't feel too good either.

"Are we… Are we still together?" she asked suddenly.

Something in my stomach twisted, and *shit*, it seriously hurt. Lauren didn't pose the question in the form of a threat, like most women I'd known. It wasn't her roundabout way of letting me know she was thinking about dropping me. She asked because she really didn't know.

And that made me feel guilty as fuck.

It was a totally valid question coming from her. I hadn't exactly been a shining example of a man in a relationship for the past few days. I was doing a piss poor job of making her feel secure and wanted.

Hell, Lauren told me she loved me, and I told her I didn't care. I couldn't even lie and say that was a mistake, because at the time—I really *didn't* care. I knew it must've broken her heart, but I had more pressing shit to attend to.

Real life ain't a movie. The world don't stop just because you love somebody.

On top of dismissing her love for me, I also allowed Lauren to think I was dead for six days. Now *that* was fucked up. I didn't have to do that. However, after everything that went down with *Poseidon* and in Memphis, I was having a strange battle of emotions. I wanted to be alone, and I *needed* her—both at the same time.

The feeling of needing someone was so foreign to me.

And so I ran from it, isolating myself right up until she showed up at my doorstep.

Growing uncomfortable in my silence, and suspecting the worse, Lauren began to put some more distance between us. Without words I reached out and stopped her as she moved, setting my hand at her waist before quietly pulling her in closer.

"Don't do that," I whispered, creating less and less space between us. *How do you even begin to tell someone that you need them? Without sounding like you're trying to guilt them into never leaving.* I kept it short and simple. "Stay."

"Stay in what? This spot, or in...*this*?" she questioned, *this* meaning *us*.

"Both," I said quietly as I touched my forehead to hers. Against her lips, I whispered, "Stay in both."

She laid there, in one of my shirts that was big enough to be a short dress on her, and eyed me with apprehension. For the first time in my life, I was the one playing games in my own relationship. This push-pull bullshit had to be annoying for her. Or, at least, frustrating.

"I'm sorry. For *everything*." Apologizing doesn't come easy for me, but when the words were for Lauren, they came out all too easy and all too often. "I know I'm being shifty, and I know it's probably got you feeling insecure as hell, but... I still want this. I still want *you*. I just—could we just erase the last seven days, and pick up where we left off before this mess started?"

That was asking for a lot.

I could tell she was thinking about me, and not her own feelings, when she nodded. "Okay."

* * *

I woke up to the sound of vacuuming downstairs.

Beside me, Lauren slept peacefully, her dark brown skin reflecting the sunlight that streamed in from outside, almost glittering. It's crazy how much you notice normally mundane shit when you're really feeling someone. Like the way sunlight turns gold against brown skin, or how hypnotizing the rise and fall of your girl's body is as she breathes.

I think I finally understand why niggas write poetry.

She didn't wake as I got out of bed, for which I was thankful. I tried to be as quiet as possible as I slipped out of my room, following the sounds coming up from down below.

Vance was in the living room, vacuum on loud, when I walked in. The red splotches on the carpet had turned a pale pink, meaning the *Resolve* powder had done its job overnight. There was an unpleasant rusty iron scent in the air, but with a little bleach, both the smell and the leftover pink stains would be gone.

"You didn't have to clean up my mess," I spoke over the loud whirring of the *Hoover*. Vance glanced at me, and waited until he was finished before acknowledging me again.

"It is almost eight o'clock in the morning," Vance informed, switching the machine off finally. "And I don't know how you like to eat your breakfast, but I can't work up an appetite in the middle of a crime scene. If you want to help, then help." He nodded towards two buckets left the base of the kitchen island for me to grab.

The plastic containers were warm to the touch, smelling strongly of *Clorox*, and inside one was about a half-dozen soaking rags. If I hadn't woken up, my uncle really would have cleaned up this entire mess for me, I realized. This was something I should've thanked him for, but instead, I was… *pissed*. There was something about his behavior that made me feel like my competence was being challenged.

It was insulting.

My uncle was locked up for twelve years. When he went away, I was eight years old. Evidently, he didn't seem to think I'd aged at all while he was gone.

"I can do this myself." Ironically, I could hear myself sounding like some kid as I tried to be a man. "I don't need your help, Vance."

"I didn't say you did." He shrugged, grabbing the bucket's handle. "But like I said, the sooner this is cleaned up, the sooner I can have breakfast. If you wanna help, then *we* can get this done faster. Grab a rag."

Vance and I had a lot in common, with one similarity being in our stubbornness. I could stand here and start a futile argument about cleaning blood out of the living room carpet because my ego was wounded, or I could grab a rag, clean up this mess with his help, and put this shit behind me once and for all.

"So, how'd you meet the girl?" Vance asked as we went to work on the biggest pink spot on the carpet. A part of me knew a conversation was coming. Vance wouldn't have passed up the opportunity.

People fresh out of prison are always trying to have long ass conversations about nothing. With so little outside experience to speak of, my guess was that they lived vicariously through the experiences of others.

I'd never given it much thought, but that might've been why I hated being around people who had recently got out. Talking just to talk had never really been my thing. But this wasn't people—this was Vance.

"I met her at a party," I replied vaguely. He didn't need to know *everything*.

"And when did you find out she was Caplan's kid?"

"Same night." I wrung out the rag into the second bucket, putting it back to soak in the bleach as I reached for another cloth. "It's complicated."

"I can keep up," Vance encouraged.

"You wouldn't get it."

"Because...?"

"I don't even get it," I confessed. "Lauren is just... You ever meet someone so good, that you feel morally obligated to keep them in one piece? It's a lot of people in the world that deserve the fucked up shit that happens on the daily. Lauren ain't one of them."

"She's Joshua Caplan's daughter," Vance reminded. "And Caplan is one of the most lowdown brothers at that courthouse. He don't care who did the crime so long as his conviction rate stays up. In case you forgot, my case was supposed to be a mistrial. And that nigga worked overtime to get a guilty verdict despite having almost no evidence. There are hundreds of innocent black men behind bars because that ruthless-ass nigga is all about his numbers. It's more than just Silas who would like to get their hands on that girl."

"You got something you want to tell me?" I waited.

"Calm down, Youngblood. I don't hurt little girls. I'm just sayin'—yeah, she may not deserve to get hurt, but her father sure does. And kids been sufferin' for the sins of their parents since the dawn of the time. It's called inherited karma."

"I don't care what it's called," I rebuffed. "And if staying outta prison was so important to you, you shouldn't have taken the fall for some shit you didn't do."

Vance paused, catching his words before they could escape. When he finally did speak again, he decided to change the subject.

"You're wasting your time trying to save this one," he said finally. "You don't understand girls like her, Youngblood."

Over the past few months, the thing I'd grown to hate the most was people trying to tell me about my own girlfriend. Amir had done it incessantly, right up until the day he died.

My stomach felt heavy with the reminder. Death is a troubling experience. It doesn't hit and stick when it's supposed to. So you're left with constant reminders. Over and over, you tell yourself this person is no longer with you, just to forget and break down all over again upon remembering.

Needing a distraction, I encouraged Vance to be a little more descriptive.

"Girls like that…" Vance sighed as if remembering something. "Girls like Lauren want the kind of things you can't give. They have ideas about how the future should be. You really think a girl like that, who grew up watching her parents playing tennis at some fancy country club somewhere, is just gonna fall into the role of a crime boss's woman? God only knows what those niggas from last night did to her, and yet she didn't even have the stomach to watch them die. She's not gonna make it out here, Youngblood."

"You're trying to talk me outta this."

"Boy, you *killed* for this girl. You *already* in this. I'm tellin' you to quit while you ahead."

"And if I say fuck all that?"

Vance chuckled to himself, cleaning away at the carpet wordlessly. It was an hour of scrubbing in silence before he finally said something.

"You'll learn the hard way."

Lauren wasn't in my bed when I arrived back in the room, but I followed the sound of running water to my bathroom, and found her brushing her teeth casually at the sink.

Her eyes glanced in my direction briefly, eyeing the orangey bleach stains on my black shirt before turning back to face her reflection in the mirror and continuing to brush without a word. Acknowledging her cold demeanor, I didn't immediately walk into the shower like I wanted to, but instead reached for my own toothbrush.

"Do you have something you wanna say to me?" I asked, squeezing some toothpaste onto the bristles. I leaned over from behind her to run my brush under the running water.

A deep V formed between her eyebrows, and I tried not to smile because she seemed genuinely angry. Lauren was amusingly cute when she was mad, though.

"You didn't have to let me think you were dead for six days," she hissed, her words coming out awkwardly as she tried to talk and brush simultaneously. Now that all the commotion from last night had died down, she was allowing the gravity of what I'd done to her set in. I was just glad she hadn't brought up my response to her first '*I love you*'.

"You're right," I agreed, and her eyes narrowed. Somehow my agreement only made her angrier. Lauren spit into the sink, making a dramatic show of keeping eye contact with me as she did it. Shaking my head at her behavior, I sighed, "It's complicated."

"I'm a smart woman," she countered.

A few weeks before, I'd let my guard all the way down with Lauren. I told her about my childhood, about Vance, about Silas, even about my nightmares. I was relieved to have gotten so much off my chest, but that didn't stop the self-loathing that consumed me immediately after I did it. All my life, I'd been taught to bite the bullet and maintain, at least, the appearance of having my shit together. Silas always said that a man who can't deal with his own problems without bitching about it is not a real man.

After *Poseidon*, and then the shit that went down in Memphis, I needed her. Not want—*need*. The grief of losing my friend coupled with the guilt of knowing I caused it, made for a toxic mix of emotions that left me feeling drained and damaged. Lauren's absence only seemed to make me feel worse, which alternatively had me considering her presence might make me feel better—thus, a need was created.

And *that* shit scared the fuck out of me. So I ran from it.

I couldn't own up to it out loud.

"It's complicated," I repeated. "But it won't happen again."

It was an empty promise. In truth, I actually couldn't be sure it wouldn't happen again. I could see in Lauren's eyes that this response didn't completely satisfy her, but she believed in my promise. For that, I made a mental note to do everything in my power to not break it.

We continued to brush in an almost comfortable silence. *Almost* comfortable.

After some time, Lauren leaned over the bathroom counter to spit into the sink again. The shirt of mine that she had on rose up slightly, exposing just a bit of the bottom half of her ass—a view I felt all the way down to my dick. I shook away the thoughts, leaning forward from behind her and aiming into the sink as she rose her head from it.

Straightening up, she backed up a little, bumping into me, and lingering for what felt like a second too long. My eyes rose lazily from the sink, catching her expression in the mirror, as she mumbled a half-assed apology and giggled. It wouldn't be the first, second, or third time I'd need to take a cold shower because Lauren was out here playing games.

Lauren is the opposite of slick. If I didn't like her so much, her easy-to-see-through antics might've started to get annoying.

"Are you *actually* hard right now?" she asked, her tone a mixture of faux surprise, teasing, and intrigue. I knew not to read too much into that last one. Lauren could be very wishy washy about sex, and I'd since learned not to let her get my hopes up.

It wasn't like me to be so gracious about getting bait-and-switched on constantly, but for Lauren, I developed the endurance. After all, our relationship literally started with me interrupting her almost-rape. The last thing I wanted to do was to ever make her feel like I was taking ownership of her body.

Even though it is mine.

The thought drew a smirk out of me as I set my toothbrush down.

"What's funny?" she asked, noting my smile.

"You're cute," I said in a way that really said, *'You think you're smooth, huh?'*

She frowned at the declaration, sighing boredly as she dragged her shirt over her head. Lauren, I'd come to learn, seemed to be pretty comfortable naked. I suspected this was because she knew her body was fucking perfect.

Lauren had a long, slender frame that pushed out at her hips, and then back in at the base of her thighs, creating this masterpiece of a figure that I'd wanted to see naked since the moment I met her. Her slim pear shape was unbelievably sexy, giving her an enigmatic allure when clothed, only to become breathtaking when seen for all it was.

Hers was the type of beauty to make a man write poems, for real.

"Who says I'm trying to be cute?" she asked coyly.

I smiled, shaking my head. *Here she goes again with that bullshit.* I'd fallen into the trap of her enticing flirtation once already. Lauren talked a big game, but she would switch up on me real quick once shit got intense. She liked to feel wanted though, and after six days of making her feel unwanted, the least I could do was gas her up.

I leaned in, keeping my voice just above a whisper at her ear when I said, "I missed you, you know that?"

She encouraged me to keep going. "What about me did you miss?"

"Everything. Your company, most of all," I replied, running a finger slowly down her spine, and noting the way it made her draw in a long inhale. "And, of course, the way you feel, the way you smell, the way you...*taste.*"

She exhaled. I cracked a half-smile, drawing back from her ear.

"I pretty much got it all back, 'cept that last one," I hinted.

Rather than say anything, she reached for the hem of my shirt, guiding it above my head. I let her, even though I was sure nothing was about to happen. Lauren liked to have her fun, and I didn't mind the view.

"Do you want me?" she asked, her voice a pitch higher than usual, vulnerable.

She, of course, had to have known the answer. I said nothing at first, sloping forward just enough for the curve her forehead to fit perfectly against the space between my lower lip and the base of my chin. As always, her hair smelled like vanilla.

She repeated herself, sincerely wanting to hear my answer.

"That's a dumb question," I replied frankly into her curls. "Which you already know the answer to."

"Do I?"

Something about that statement stung like hundreds of little needles pressed into my skin. Lauren chuckled to herself with little to no humor.

"What's on your mind?" I asked curiously. She drew her head back, eying me with a vaguely amused smile, her cute as hell dimples prominent.

"You're still hard," she marveled as if this was unbelievable.

"Lauren, you are butt ass naked."

"Wanna join me?" Her fingers settled at the waistband of my gray sweats, eyes coming up to mine with a silent urge for permission. I didn't stop her as she tugged them down, watching as her front teeth sunk into her lower lip slowly. My erection twitched at the sight. There was just something about the way Lauren would bite that lip of hers. She asked again, "Do you want me?"

What a strange question to ask a man you've got hard as fuck without even touching.

"Clearly," I replied. "I do."

Her arms at my abdomen rose to circle around my neck, pulling me along as she stepped backwards toward the shower. Looking over her shoulder, she moved one arm behind her for the faucet, the steady rhythm of her breathing growing irregular as the running water warmed over her outstretched hand.

She was nervous.

And *this* was when I realized Lauren was not playing with me. Not this time. Rather than excite me, this concerned me at first.

"Hey," I called her attention away from the running water, raising my eyebrows questioningly once she looked my way. "Where's all this comin' from?"

"I want you, as well," she explained in the exact same tone you'd expect someone to say, 'Duhh, *obviously*'.

"Yeah, but—"

"Stop talking," she complained, stepping backward into the glass-walled shower, until the water landed on her shoulders. Her hands landed in mine and pulled me forward. "Don't try to talk me out of this."

The shrinking distance between us was tempting. As the space between her lips and mine came to a close, my inhibitions moved to the far, far corners of my mind, unleashing a lust from within that decided to ignore the red flags. Something was definitely wrong, but once Lauren's lips were on mine, all of those thoughts left my immediate attention.

Lauren's first few kisses were shy, testing the waters as she got a feel for how much the time apart might've changed our relationship. As she realized our dynamic was left unchanged, her arms came up and circled around my neck, pulling my body in closer, her hardened nipples pressing into my chest. I kissed her back, a mere participant at first, rather than take over, giving her the opportunity to find her own, to get comfortable.

Kissing Lauren was always an event.

Even though she'd gained a lot of experience with me these last few months, it was always a cat and mouse chase with her. Initially, she would come in aggressively, and then draw back shyly before she got carried away. I doubted she knew her habit of doing this drove me insane. Not in a bad way, of course. Lauren's natural tendency to tease gave my natural tendency to dominate something to work towards.

Her initial aggressiveness subsided and like clockwork, I started to feel her reeling back.

No you won't...

I followed her as she drew back, my hand coming around between her shoulder blades and holding her in place. Her muscles relaxed as I took over, matching my momentum as I took lead. It was with subtle intrigue that I noted that although the water that poured over us was hot, Lauren's nipples against me were rock hard. My mouth followed hers as she took a few steps back, ultimately stopping once her backside pressed against the marble ledge mounted against the shower's back wall. Bottles of shower gel and shampoo fell from it, slamming into the puddles at our feet.

Without our lips separating, she hopped onto the built-in shower ledge for a seat, and her hand dropped down to take me within her grasp. Slowly, her hand moved up and down my length, a kind of uncertainty in her touch. It was then that my lips moved away from hers, and just like the last time we tried this, I offered her an out.

"Are you good?" My voice was hoarse, which took her (and me) by surprise. But *goddamn*... the feel of her hand moving up and down the length of my erection was intense—unexpectedly intense. After being in a monogamous relationship with a woman like Lauren, caught up in the enjoyment of simply being around her, it seemed to have slipped my mind that I hadn't physically been with anyone in months.

Months. I'd been celibate for over a hundred and ten days.

How the hell did I not notice?

Lauren's eyes rose to mine slowly from where she sat, answering my question not with words, but in the way her hand came around my back and pulled me in closer as she wordlessly spread her thighs.

Lauren talks when she's nervous.

Today, she didn't say a word. Ironically, her uncharacteristic silence only seemed to draw out the talkativeness in me. When my voice sounded in my ears, it almost sounded like I was trying to talk her out of it. I couldn't explain it, but something just didn't feel right.

"I don't have protection."

Lauren's eyes dragged back up, peering through her eyelashes when she replied, "Do you have anything I could catch?"

I made a face at first, stating the obvious, "A baby probably."

She chuckled at this answer, flashing a coquettish smile that was doing absolutely nothing to calm my erection down. "That's what the morning after pill is for."

No sign of humor in her words.

She pulled me in closer, craning her neck for a kiss which I unreservedly gave. In the middle of the kiss, Lauren scooted up a little from her seat, touching the head of my shaft lightly against the plumper folds of her opening. In that moment, there was absolutely no going back. A sound like a moan reverberated through her lips against mine in response to the new sensation.

I didn't part my lips from her, keeping her attention as my hand traveled down to guide myself through the distance that separated us once and for all. The last time I'd been with a virgin, I was a virgin myself, and if my memory served correctly, there was nothing I could do to make this totally comfortable for her.

But I could try my best.

The water from the shower hit along my back, traveling down the rest of my body and hers. Lauren was so wet that she was overflowing, and that had nothing to do with the shower stream. As I moved the tip of my erection up and down the length of her folds, coating myself with her natural juices, the water from the shower mixed in to create more slip.

With her hands still set on my back, our lips briefly separated, and she drew in one breath before I brought it right back, pushing into her at the exact moment our lips touched.

Lauren flinched, her teeth sinking into my lower lip involuntarily in response to the initial discomfort. Behind me, I felt her fingernails dig so deeply into my back that I was sure she was puncturing the skin. I paused for a stretched moment, allowing some time for her to get acclimated to my girth. From the way I felt each and every contour of her warm walls cling along the rigid hardness of my erection, I knew one thing for sure.

The tremendously tight fit was incredible for me, but for her it must've felt like I was ripping her in half. Slowly, I inched further into her, feeling her fingernails drag down my back in one long, painful scratch. I didn't mind, as I was aware that I was likely hurting her more than she was hurting me. Three quarters of the way in, the force of her grip relaxed slowly, a sign that the hardest part was beginning to pass.

Drawing back, I eyed her curiously as I ran my tongue along the part of my lip where she'd bitten me. I tasted blood, which for some reason, I found funny. Neither of us said anything, and the stream from the shower poured on, hitting us both. It was then that I made a decision, realizing where I was.

"Wrap your legs around my waist," I instructed, my voice coming out husky—completely lost in the moment. To her questioning eyes, I explained, "We're not doin' this here."

My girl's first time is not gonna be in a shower.

Lauren's wet hair set along my pillows, encircling her head like a curly, black saint's halo. Her back pressed into my bed, the tiny droplets of water on her naked skin running down to meet the fabric of my sheets. She looked at me with those dark eyes wide with expectation, as I hovered over her, feeling her walls tense up around me with every breath I took.

"Relax," I whispered, trying to sound reassuring, but against the intensity of her tight hold on me, the word barely came out audible. Still, she somehow understood, letting out a slow breath before grazing her front teeth along her lower lip nervously. *Lauren and that lip*...

My dick twitched at the sight. I'd never actually told her that watching her bite that lower lip of hers never failed to turn me on, but she'd certainly felt my response to it just then. A half smile raised my cheek as I lowered down to meet her lips, timing my first thrust at the exact moment our lips touched.

As expected, she flinched, her hand coming up to catch my bicep reflexively before relaxing yet again. I deepened our kiss, starting my movements off slow so to not hurt her, developing a slow and deliberate momentum that saw her fingernails squeeze into my arm. Lauren, despite her expected discomfort, was into it. I could tell from how wet she was. With each thrust into her, I felt her fingers around my arm loosen, and the rigidity of her body relax once and for all.

Briefly, I thought myself lucky for the fact that I wouldn't need to pull out. I was sure I didn't have the willpower.

When the first moan passed through her lips, it marked a meaningful transition in the process. As her pain began to subside, I could feel the composition of her body change the moment it started to get good for her. I smiled against her lips, a sense of relief settling upon confirming I hadn't hurt her too bad. That was my cue to up my speed, at the same time bringing my hand down between us to meet her clit, as I gradually increased my pace. At the first hint of my fingers rubbing into her spot, her walls involuntarily clenched harder onto my dick. Our lips parted, and a whine sounding like my name echoed through the room.

Shit.

She was perfect.

I'd never been one of those '*Say my name*,' type niggas in bed, but with Lauren, hearing my name scattered along sounds of her labored breaths between each moan was—

"Kaaaaain!"

Beautiful.

Lauren's body quaked under mine, her fingernails digging into my skin once again, but this time for a different reason. Her breath hitched, the hardened nipples of her breasts pausing against me, and for a brief second, everything stopped. To the cadence of the most beautiful moan, I felt her arms wrap around my neck, pulling me down for another kiss as her body rocked to the rhythm of the first orgasm.

"I love you," she confessed between kisses, her voice sounding like a cry, weakened and quick as though she had no intention of hearing me say it back. "I love you so much, Kain."

Lauren didn't wait for a reaction, giving me no room for comment in the way that she desperately pulled me back down to her. There was a necessity in her behavior, an undeniable need to be close as her second orgasm shot through her and prompted her legs to come around and pin me to her.

The intense clenching of her vaginal muscles as she climaxed and quivered was just what it took to set me over my own threshold. A guttural sound that almost sounded pained ripped from me as I filled her with my seed, a seemingly never-ending supply, as one of the most intense orgasms I'd ever experienced took complete control over me.

Lauren's breathing was erratic as she struggled to catch it, her hold on my arms growing limp as her dark eyes fluttered open to meet mine. The euphoric look on her face was a relief to me as I came down from my own personal high.

I didn't ruin her first time. There had been an inexplicable fear in me that I'd misstep and do something that would scar her. Seeing the faint smile in her eyes now turned out to be the most satisfying part of this entire experience.

I watched as her teeth sunk into that lower lip yet again—a sign that she was nervous. Despite this, Lauren was the first to say something. As we laid side by side, watching each other affectionately, her feather light voice chimed.

"Please don't ever leave me again."

Again.

As my mind began to clear, it was then that I understood what just happened. Lauren didn't give her innocence to me just now—she *surrendered* it. A last ditch bargaining tool, so that I could make her a promise and calm her insecurities. In exchange for her all, she asked that I don't break her heart ever again. She felt unsafe in my arms now. She felt temporary.

And her body was all she believed she had to offer. Her virginity.

Shit.

The last thing I wanted to happen, happened. I did ruin her first time.

With six words, Lauren filled me with a regret that shattered me inside. I didn't wear the heartbreak on my face at first, opting to wordlessly pull her close, both as a silent reassurance and so that she wouldn't see the guilt that flashed through my eyes.

"I'm yours," I confessed, the most vulnerable thing I'd ever said out loud to anyone. "Long before today, and long after it—I'm yours."

Lauren pulled away from my grasp, compelled to look into my eyes for signs of dishonesty. She searched them for what felt like ages.

When she confirmed my words to be true, she replied, "Promise me."

The faint smile that turned up my cheek was vaguely sad. I had her love, but I did not have her trust.

"I promise."

Chapter Six

KAIN

For the next seven days, Lauren was careful—or rather, *uncomfortable*—around me. She didn't speak too loud; she didn't move too suddenly. Seven days of my girlfriend doing her absolute best to fade into the background of my days. She apologized for things she never used to apologize for; she asked for permission for things she once upon a time did freely.

On the first day, I got her as far away from my father's home as soon as I could. She was quiet the entire ride over, fidgeting with her fingers in a way I'd never seen her do. When we'd arrived at the safe house, she eyed the interior as if she could see earlier versions of ourselves haunting throughout. She was reliving a simpler time, an air of nostalgia in her features, a desire for that simplicity once more. I wished I could've given it to her.

On the second day, we went to the nearest pharmacy so that Lauren could pick up Plan B emergency birth control. When the cashier had asked her for ID, she didn't have it.

"I don't have my ID," she'd said, her voice sounding small, embarrassed. I couldn't be sure if she was uncomfortable because the woman behind the counter was all too aware of what we'd done, or if it was because she felt foolish for having thought she could buy the emergency pill without proving she was an adult. Either way, this was nothing to be self-conscious about.

"I've got it," I interjected, pulling out my driver's license. The cashier's attention settled on me and between her deep set eyes, a hard line V creased with outrage. *So* you're *the nigga who recklessly came up in this sweet-faced girl*, her look conveyed. I reminded her that she had a job to do. "Ring me up."

Lauren sat at the foot of our bed once we'd arrived and settled back home. She read the back of the box over and over again, repeatedly expressing anxiety over the side effects listed on the back.

"I once read an article that said frequent use of emergency contraceptives leads to infertility."

I'd met the worry in her eyes, and sighed.

"It's girls out here popping Plan B's like vitamins every weekend. You've got nothing to worry about, and this isn't about to be a recurring thing for us."

Her face fell, a misunderstanding of my words. Clearly, she was still insecure about the nature of our relationship if she took my words to mean that I had no intention of touching her ever again. What I meant was that next time we took it there, either I'd suit up, or she'd be on regular birth control. I clarified this, annoyed that I even needed to, but patient.

"Oh," was all she whispered, rising to her feet and slipping past me. "I'm gonna go get a glass of water from the kitchen."

Days three through seven passed without incident. Most of her bruises had cleared, and Lauren and I kept conversations surface level. I didn't ask her about her parents, and she didn't ask me about Amir. Those were two elephants in the room, breathing heavily and begging to be addressed. When Friday morning came, my elephant grew too big to ignore.

"His funeral is tomorrow," I announced at breakfast, watching as Lauren's spoonful of oatmeal stopped halfway to her mouth. She set the spoon down, eyes staring a hole through mine. I'd addressed my elephant. I was finally talking about him and mixed in with the shock in her features, there was some relief there, too. I wasn't completely scattered in the wind, she concluded. "I don't know if it's even right that I go."

Lauren cleared her throat, thrown by the suddenness of my vulnerability. I, too, realized that a Friday morning breakfast was a bit of an unexpected time to lay my problems at her feet. But Lauren, as strange as it sounded, welcomed signs of weakness in me like no one else could. Strange as it may have seemed, I felt oddly safe in her presence. So for her, I would let my guard down from time to time. For her, I could cut the act.

"You'll regret it if you don't go." She was absolutely right.

"I know."

"It's just…" I sighed, shaking my head resignedly. There were no words for the lurch in my stomach. *What does a cringe sound like?* "It's hard not to feel like I'll be that nigga who shows up to bury the man he killed."

"You didn't kill him."

I only looked at her, a skeptical crease forming between my brows. Lauren and I both knew Amir would still be alive today if not for my requests of him. She herself had been there when Amir and I shook on it.

"I didn't pull the trigger," I amended. "But I might as well have."

"The blame game is all about varying degrees of association," she shrugged. I eyed her with confusion, inviting her to explain that. "What if Silas hadn't killed your cousin? What if it hadn't rained that night, and traffic was a little better? What if I didn't try to stop you when you left? What if—"

"Don't." I raised a hand to stop her. "I've already been through all of the what-ifs. Thinking of you, and not me, as the reason Amir might be dead will not help."

"I'm just saying you can make anything anyone's fault if you look at situations from different directions."

"Yeah, I know," I replied dismissively. "But join me in skipping the ones that place the blame on yourself."

"But you won't extend yourself that same courtesy."

"I don't need to," I replied.

"And you *need* to do so for me?" she posed skeptically.

"As a matter of fact, I do."

"Why?"

In the haste of the back and forth, I confessed, "Because I don't want to hate you."

Lauren swallowed her words back down. She had nothing to say now, but I had something to add.

"Because my best friend is dead, and the last person I want to blame is my other best friend."

Her eyes raised from her bowl of oatmeal, eyes watering a little at the sound of that admission. God, I hated to see her cry. Only this time, I wasn't sure if her tears were of sadness or of relief.

Her voice was croaky when she spoke again, "I think you should go to the funeral, Kain."

"Only if... Only if you come with me." Vulnerability fit me like a pair of shoes two sizes too small. I knew all the risks that came with being somewhere so public with Lauren Caplan, but after everything that happened in the past few weeks, it was only a matter of time before Silas found out about our relationship.

Lauren was genuinely taken aback by my request. "You want me there?"

A humorless chuckled rumbled up from my chest, and I shook my head at the question. Not because my answer was no, but because her asking it only served to show me that she had absolutely no idea. No idea at all...

"Lauren..." The words weighed heavy on my tongue, threatening to shatter my teeth on their way out. This was so hard for me to admit. Not because I was ashamed, but because admitting it went against everything I'd been taught since birth. Silas always used to say, the minute you *need* anything or anyone, it's over. "Baby... I need you there."

* * *

In Ghana, where my deceased friend was born, the colors of mourning are black for the grief, and red for the danger. Because of the nature of Amir's death, naturally, the crowd at the church was a sea of red. At the moment I stepped through the threshold, the wave-like commotion among them seemed to hush into a complete silence. One by one, conversations abruptly ended and heads turned.

I was easily able to ignore the hateful looks from those around me. No one would say anything to my face. Funeral or not—I was *still* Kain Montgomery, and nobody wants a Montgomery for an enemy. My eyes could only zero in on the closed cherry wood casket adorned with flowers at the pulpit. Amir was in there, cold and lifeless, above ground for just a few short hours before finally leaving us in symbolic completion. As expected, even though I was devastated, my eyes did not water.

I wasn't one for crying over much of anything.

In the eerie silence of the church, Lauren's hand found mine, squeezing my palm reassuringly. My eyes traveled up the red fabric of Lauren's red dress—Lauren in red was always a beautiful sight—and met her watering eyes.

Wow, I thought to myself.

Lauren, a girl who'd known Amir all of four months could muster up the emotion it took to shed tears in the midst of his closed casket. And me? I had nothing but a downcast expression and an overwhelming feeling of guilt to offer my best friend of nearly fifteen years.

The sermon droned on, a bizarrely religious ceremony for someone like Amir whose faith never stretched beyond a '*bless you*' post sneeze when he was alive. The sounds of women—family and friends of his—crying in the church bounced off the walls like a choir of sniffles and whimpers accompanying the booming voice of the pastor. I could feel dozens of eyes burning holes into the back of my suit. It was oddly satisfying to be around people who blamed me just as much as I blamed myself.

When it came time for any friends of Amir to speak, a few heads turned my way, but I didn't budge. What would I say? Again, Lauren squeezed my hand to remind me that she was here for me. It was without question that this ceremony would've been unbearable had she not been here. One by one, we watched people who didn't know Amir as much as I did take the stage and say their peace. It grated on my nerves to have to sit through all of it, easily picking out the things that weren't true, or the things he wouldn't have wanted said.

It was only then that I realized that neither Marlon or Jay were present. This somewhat made sense. Closed-casket funerals are nothing but torture for the living—no sense of closure from a last look before saying goodbye forever.

The last person to speak was probably the only person in the room who knew Amir better than I did. Cierra, Amir's girlfriend. Cierra, my sister.

Her fingers tightened around the mic as she tried to gain control of her breathing, looking at the floor as she spoke.

"I used to call him Mir." A sob clamored from out of her chest. "I was the only one who called him that. He used to answer to it with the biggest smile on his face and just reply, '*What is it, my love?*'" She chuckled a humorless laugh and wiped at her cheeks. "Not many people know that. Amir was such a soft and caring soul. So special. He loved hard, and I loved him back."

My sister took a moment to get control of her emotions.

"I feel like a part of my heart was ripped out of my chest, and some days I swear it hurts to breathe. I miss him every second of every day, and when I talk to him in my mind, all of our conversations start with, '*What is it, my love?*', and to that I say… I say I hope I wake up from this nightmare."

Lauren's hand came up to catch the tears she shed for my sister, a slight movement that called Cierra's attention her way. Cierra's pained eyes darkened at the sight of my girlfriend's tears. There was venom in her gaze that pierced through Lauren as if she were looking directly at Amir's killer in the flesh. It occurred to me that this was because as far as Cierra was concerned—she *was* looking at Amir's killer.

Or at least the reason he was dead.

From Lauren, Cierra's eyes traveled to me, and with a simple look—I just knew. Cierra wasn't just sad.

She was pissed.

Chapter Seven

KAIN

"Kain, you have no shame."

Cierra's voice was a hiss as the funeral guests began to disperse. We were at the cemetery, the air smelling of freshly dug earth, decaying flowers, and rain. After laying my best friend to rest and saying my final farewell, I wasn't in the mood to receive whatever tongue lashing my sister was about to dish out. Almost instinctively, I pulled Lauren's hand back and positioned her behind me. Cierra's whole demeanor was wild aggressive, and I wasn't taking any chances.

"You brought *her* to the funeral," my sister observed incredulously. There was malice in her eyes, clashing with the grief. "Hell, you thought it would be alright if even *you* came?"

"Ci, I'm not doing this here." My whispered response did not deter her.

With a raised dismissive hand, Cierra informed, "I figured it out."

Her eyes zeroed in on my girl, narrowing slightly in a way that fired up the protectiveness in me.

"Cierra…" There was an edge of warning in my tone.

"I figured it out," she repeated, tilting her head to the side and shaking it slightly. "Your girlfriend—she's not some police officer's daughter. It worse than that. That's why you put Amir's life on the line—to protect your secret."

I turned to Lauren and handed her the keys to my car, urging her to go with a nod.

"I'm right behind you," I promised. She eyed me warily, only creating some distance between us when I urged her a little more.

"You two headed to the house in Pembroke Pines?" Cierra questioned, her mouth twisting in a triumphant scowl. I was surprised to learn that my sister knew about it, but at the same time, I wasn't surprised at all. Amir had been the one who'd sold me that house. It made a lot of sense for Cierra to know about it. When he was alive, Cierra had Amir wrapped around her finger. "Yeah, Amir told me about the house back when it was supposed to be for Vance, but since he never moved in, I can only assume it's been where you've been hiding with your b—"

"Don't test me, Ci," I cut her off just before she could call Lauren out her name. "I get that you're upset, and I—"

"Save me the bullshit condolences, Kain." She lifted a hand. "You're fucking the daughter of the man trying to put Daddy in prison. You're shameless. Despicable. I can't believe you."

I sighed. "Are you done?"

"You sacrificed your best friend—*my* best friend—to be with that *trick*!" Cierra wiped at the tears falling from her eyes roughly. Her tears were the only thing keeping me from checking her. *Time and place*, I acknowledged. "I won't let you sacrifice Daddy, too. I won't let you."

She was inconsolable.

And that was a threat.

One that I caught on to rather quickly.

"Cierra, before you—"

She forced out a humorless laugh, shaking her head. "I already did. Daddy's flying in from Memphis as we speak."

＊ ＊ ＊

The lobby of the Bayside Hotel was washed in luminously bright lighting that reflected in the dark brown color of Lauren's eyes as she eyed the five-star Downtown Miami building with awe. The wonderment in her features made something in my chest swell, I noted, with a faint smile.

Lauren was the perfect combination of beautiful and infectiously cute. What with her big eyes and dimpled cheeks, one couldn't help but meet the urge to reach out and touch her every once in a while. I certainly couldn't, my thumb grazing the soft skin of her face in admiration.

The man behind the check-in counter cleared his throat once, trying to draw my attention away from my girl and at him. Reluctantly I turned, reading out the reservation I'd placed only minutes before on my phone in the parking lot outside.

"Montgomery." I nodded toward his computer for him to check for my name. When his gaze brushed over the scale of the room I'd booked, I watched his eyebrows raise first in surprise, and then lower with suspicion.

Here we go...

"Presidential suite?" he tried to confirm the room, taking on a tone as though unsure he was reading the correct reservation off the screen. As a very young man with a lot of money at my disposal, it was all too common for me to be met with this kind of skepticism. I simply nodded, too tired and stressed out by the earlier events of today to get irritated. "And how long will you be staying?"

"Indefinitely," I replied, and to his look of uncertainty, I sighed and clarified, "A while. Put me in for a month for now."

"The room is eight thousand per night," he made sure to inform as if I didn't already know this.

I was losing my patience and I knew the shoes on Lauren's feet were uncomfortable. "And?"

"A month-long stay will be—"

"I did the math," I interrupted, pulling out my black American Express. "I need two card keys, and for you to hurry this up."

The house in Pembroke Pines was no longer a safe place for Lauren to be. My sister Cierra, blinded by grief and anger, had finally blown the lid off the extensive game of hide and seek Lauren and I had been playing with Silas for the past four months. Knowing my father, now that he had an address, I wouldn't be surprised if there was someone at the house waiting for us now.

So we didn't go back.

Lauren stepped around the living room area of the Bayside Hotel presidential suite, saying nothing. If she was stressed, I certainly couldn't tell from the collected demeanor in her stride. Instead, she plopped herself down onto a loveseat, letting out a tired sigh before pulling her eyes to meet mine wordlessly.

I stood at the foyer of the suite, a large space that was structured like a one-bedroom apartment, eyeing the kitchen area that blended into a small dining room, before becoming a living room, which was just off a private bedroom.

This will do for now.

"You're still standing by the door," Lauren observed, an uncomfortable quality to her voice, coming to the realization that I wasn't staying with her. This only served to remind me that my girl rarely ever missed anything when it came to me.

I pulled my wrist up, checking the time on my *Hublot,* deciding to stay another half hour. A private flight from Memphis to Miami would be a little over two hours. Experience had told me it was better to meet my father than to let him find me. Most of all, I needed to put some distance between Lauren and me for the night.

Now that Silas knew I was with her and—
depending on how much Amir told Cierra—knew how long our relationship had been going on, I knew for a fact Lauren had just fallen on my father's list of priorities. Silas could give a damn about a Lauren Caplan now. He had a more pressing target to get a hold of right now.

Me.

For months, being by my side was the safest place for Lauren to be. But now, until I had a much needed conversation with my father, my side was the worst place for her to stay. I took a seat beside her, extending out an arm for her to fall into before tightening it around her.

"I have to go do some things back at the house, so I'm gonna step out in a few," I explained, resting my chin at the top of her hair. As always, the vanilla scent of her curls was therapeutic.

"Which house?"

"Both of them." She turned her head and looked up at me from my shoulder. There was apprehension in her eyes. "Do you have anything at the Pembroke house you want me to bring back?"

She shrugged. "Bring back when exactly?"

Tough question. I was honest with her.

"Hopefully tomorrow."

"Hopefully?"

"I don't know if I'll be back tomorrow, but I'll try." I tucked a bent finger under her chin and promised, "I'll really try."

"Will you call me after you talk to your father?" she asked, tossing a glance to the in-room landline. I nodded, making a mental note to write down the hotel room's number. "Worst case scenario, what will he do to you for this?"

"I'm honestly not sure," I replied. "I've never really crossed him like this before."

Her voice was hoarse when she forced out, "Are you scared?"

"No." This was the truth. "It's a conversation that I knew was coming. Are you scared?"

Of course, she nodded. "Sorry, I've been trying to woman up and—"

"You don't need to be sorry. Just tell me why you're scared."

Lauren pushed out a sigh before shrugging. "What if you don't come back?"

I cracked a smile at this. "Lauren."

"What?"

With a shake of my head, I reminded her of the obvious. "He's my father."

Chapter Eight

KAIN

"Silas is gonna have a stroke when he finds out about you and ol' girl." Amir tossed a judgmental look my way before adding, "I can't believe you choosing pussy over family."

The fact that I'd been with Lauren for about three months now and hadn't been intimate with her was none of Amir's business, so I didn't all the way correct him. Instead, I was fairly vague.

"Nobody's choosin' pussy over family."

"Okay," Amir hit back sarcastically, unconvinced. "You got one job to do. You take money from one place and drop it off at another. Your Pops don't ask you for nothin' else—" The dozens of texts in my phone said otherwise, but I let Amir make his point. "—and you can't even do that."

"It's just for one night."

"You say that now," he challenged. I didn't know it then, but he was absolutely right. I would be asking him to make the *Poseidon* drop one more time, and that would ultimately be the favor that got him killed. "You trustin' a nigga with almost four hundred Gs of your father's money because what? You wanna take some prissy rich girl to a shooting range? What kind of corny shit is that?"

"Oh, that's why you don't like her? Because you think she's prissy."

"Nah, I didn't say I didn't like her," Amir corrected, using his nickname for her as he explained, "Princess is a good kid. If she was fuckin' around with Marlon or Jay, it'd be an odd match, but I wouldn't have shit to say about it. But it's you two—the most reckless combination I've ever seen. I have to keep remindin' myself you ain't gone crazy."

"C'mon, you know me better than that."

"Yeah! I do. And that girl... Y'all don't match. That girl is making you soft."

I raised a skeptical brow, laughing a little. "You really think so?"

"You don't?"

I shook my head. "I think you're confusing my being happier for me gettin' weak."

"Aww, you happy?" he responded mockingly. "Well let's see how happy your ass stays when you get either yourself or that girl killed." To my frown, he added, "You and I both know that if Silas doesn't have a stroke first, he's gonna kill somebody over all of this."

Saturday, June 25th, 2016
(Present Day)

The thick smell of marijuana smoke was the first thing to greet me when I shut the front door of my childhood home. For as long as I could remember, whenever my father got especially angry, the smell of weed was sure to follow. Today was no different, it seemed.

Weed calmed Silas down—his temper *and* his blood pressure.

My tense shoulders slumped downward, relaxing a bit because if ever there was a version of Silas I wanted to argue with, it was the high version. The sounds of the TV coming from the living room guided my steps further into the house, my movements deliberate, cautious. This was uncharted territory and I wasn't about to rush into it. That's how you get run up on. Another lesson learned from my father.

Vance was sitting alone in the living room when I walked in, a half smoked blunt in his hands and eyes that said, *'Shit, Youngblood, you're a dead man, you know?'*

"*Shit*, Youngblood—" my uncle started to say before I lifted a hand.

"I know... I know... I'm a dead man."

I tossed a glance over my shoulder, scanning the living room behind me, my eyes brushing over the spotless white carpet where two dead men had been laid out only a week before. Humorlessly, I chuckled, wondering if I really was next. Silas could be pretty unpredictable when he wanted to be.

"Where he at?"

Vance reached for the remote, pressing the mute button before answering my question. "He came, dismissed all the staff for the rest of the day, and waited for you."

Dismissed the staff… Whatever my father was initially planning, he didn't want witnesses.

"How long did he wait?" I asked.

"About ten minutes."

"And then?"

"He bounced, and went looking for you himself."

I thought about Lauren holed up in the presidential suite at the *Bayside*. Even though I knew it was virtually impossible for Silas to get his hands on her where she was, that didn't stop the tightening in my throat when I asked, "Did he say where he was gonna look?"

"Silas said Cierra told him you bought a house out in Broward County." Vance raised an eyebrow before asking, "You didn't leave ole girl there by herself, did you?"

Vance's tone was almost concerned. In typical Lauren fashion, she was apparently able to make my indifferent uncle care about her wellbeing without much effort. She was just that kind of girl—the type of girl you couldn't help but protect.

"She's not there," was all I said, still unsure if I could trust anyone with her whereabouts. Getting Lauren as far as possible from the house in Pembroke Pines was the first thing I did as soon as I realized that Silas knew about both it and her.

Vance brought the blunt to his mouth and nodded before asking, "You know what you're doing, Youngblood?"

I stretched out a hand for him to pass the joint, waiting for it to be in my hand before I replied, "No idea."

"You don't look stressed, though," Vance observed.

I took a long drag, shaking my head within the cloud of smoke I created. "Silas is gonna do what Silas is gonna do."

"And that is...?" my uncle asked. *Hell if I know.*

"You tell me," I responded, handing back the joint before asking, "If I was your son, and you found out I was dating the daughter of the man tryna put you away forever, and thus sabotaging your efforts to interfere with his case, what would you do?"

"I think what I would do and what Silas would do are two entirely different answers, kid."

"Be Silas then. Use your imagination."

Vance chuckled, thinking it through before finally deciding, "He just might kill your ass."

"This should be interesting then."

"Why? You got a death wish?"

"No." I shook my head, taking a seat on the sectional and checking the time on my watch. "I told her I'd be back. And I have every intention of doing that."

It was hours before Silas returned. I was just beginning to naturally slip out of my weed-induced haze when the sound of the front door slamming echoed throughout the house, sending my senses into a frenzy. I breathed out a calming breath, tossing a cursory glance Vance's way. He was already looking at me, expression neutral if not almost entertained. He was curious to see how I was gonna talk my way out of this.

Not that I would need his help, but somehow without there ever being a verbal agreement, I already knew whose side Vance was on.

"KAIN!!!!"

"Oh yeah, he's big mad," Vance mumbled more to himself than to me as he flicked through the channels on the living room television. I could've smiled at this if I was in the smiling mood.

"I'm in the living room!" I called back, not bothering to move from my comfortable position on the sectional. Vance swallowed a laugh, tossing a look my way that said 'Nigga, you got a lotta nerve.'

"I DON'T GIVE A FUCK WHERE YOU ARE!" Silas was heard (loudly), but not seen. "I'm in my office! Move your ass on."

I rose to my feet calmly, shooting Vance a lazy salute before moving past the kitchen and toward the back of the house where Silas' wing was. My pulse was normal, nothing out of the ordinary. I hadn't been afraid of my father since I was eleven. Everything I did since, I did out of obligatory respect; no more, no less.

Silas had to have known this. I wasn't exactly putting up a front; I'd never felt the need to. In a way, I always got the sense that the absence of fear in my interactions with my father was a source of pride for him. If nothing else, it showed him that he'd successfully raised a man. Once upon a time, I believe this would've been something he felt accomplished for.

However, after stepping into his office and coming face-to-face with his rage-filled eyes, I could see that what was once a source of pride for him was now presenting itself as a problem. One of the cornerstones of control is fear. People who don't fear you cannot be controlled.

Still, you couldn't raise a man and then expect him to not think for himself.

I did a lot of that.

One look at me, and he knew immediately that I wasn't sorry, and I would die before I apologized for protecting her.

I shut the door behind me, a gesture I did absentmindedly. To me, it was nothing but a closed door. To Silas, however, it was an unspoken declaration that basically said, '*I ain't scared of you, man.*'

The silence among us felt years long as my father just looked at me, eyes almost unrecognizing, as if he wasn't sure he knew the person standing in front of him anymore. His face was like mine, but weathered against the effects of time, older. I'd gotten everything from my father except for my eyes. Mine were an unusual shade of brown-gold, which I assumed came from my mother. All my life, the fact that I was the only one in my family with this color told me that I at least got something from her side; it told me that she existed once upon a time.

Without a word, the crease between Silas' brows relaxed and he leaned back in his seat, pulling in a long breath before reaching for the glass cabinet behind his head.

"Sit down," Silas ordered tiredly, pulling out two glasses and an aged bottle of cognac.

"I can stand—"

"I didn't ask you what you can fuckin' do. I said *sit down*." Silas motioned toward the chair opposite the front of his desk. Evidently he was about to lecture me Principals office-style—except with cognac. As I reached for the seat, Silas reached for the door of the miniature refrigerator under his desk, pulling out a bowl of ice chunks. He poured the several-year-old brown liquor into a glass for me before pouring one for himself, pouring a little more liberally into his own glass. "You been smoking weed with Vance?" he asked.

I reached for the glass of cognac in front of me, holding it to allow some of the ice to melt a little. "A little."

"So you good and relaxed, huh?"

"You could say that."

"So let's have a talk." Silas took a drink and sighed. "You a very good liar, Kain."

"You think so?" I posited, downing some of the alcohol in my glass.

My father nodded. "And stone cold, too."

"Hmm," I considered.

"Yeah." Silas leaned back in his seat and eyed me carefully before he concluded, "It was you."

I only stared back.

"You let me kill Sabrina, thinking she was the one who tipped Caplan off to the hit on him last spring, but it was you. Sabrina had kids, Kain."

"Sabrina also told you a dozen times that it wasn't her before you shot her."

Silas slammed his glass on the desk, his anger getting the best of him. "Yeah, but it was either her or you, and at the time, I thought ain't no way. Not my son."

"You didn't have to kill her. That's on you, not me," I replied, although deep down I did take responsibility for Sabrina's death.

When I told Lauren about the planned hit on her father last spring, Sabrina, a security guard at the courthouse, was the person who Silas ultimately zeroed in on as the rat. I never told Lauren because I didn't want her to carry the guilt that I carried, knowing four kids lost their mother over some shit I did.

"That's what we do around here, Kain," Silas exclaimed. "We kill snitches."

The way he looked at me as he said that last word was enough for me to know he was branding me as such in his mind.

In spite of myself, I laughed a little, taking a drink before replying, "Sometimes."

"The fuck is that supposed to mean?"

"Sometimes we just kill mothers with kids—like Sabrina. Hell, sometimes we even kill their kids and then kill them for feelin' some type of way about it," I alluded to Laz and Rochelle. "Sometimes we even try to kill young girls for no other reason than sending cautionary messages to their fathers."

A flash of understanding crossed my father's features. "Ahh, now we gettin' to the root of the issue—that girl. Caplan's daughter."

"My girlfriend," I unreservedly claimed her.

Silas nodded and unsurprisingly reduced her to, "Pussy."

The word clamored through his teeth insultingly, like a bark.

"I raised you for eighteen years and handed over every penny I have to you! And for that, you *spit* in my face in the name of *pussy*!" Silas poured himself another drink, his hands slightly shaking while he tried to keep the rage bubbling within him under control. "Kain, you done lost your *goddamn* mind!"

"You lost yours first."

"The fuck did you just say to me?"

"You put out a bounty for a nineteen-year-old girl! As harmless as they come, too. And for what? Because the state is taking you to trial for a case you're gonna beat anyway? At this rate, you wanna kill her just to say you did. For sport! You sick ass mothafuc—"

"*Watch your fuckin' mouth.*" He got parental on me, adding in a less than parental threat, "Don't let that alcohol get you bodied. And you right. I might've wanted her *just* so I could wipe that smug ass look off of that nigga Joshua Caplan's face." My father took a drink before concluding, "But now I want her 'cause she knows too fuckin' much."

"Which is what exactly?"

"You tell me, Kain." Silas looked at me expectantly. "You the one that's been shackin' up with her. Y'all two are real close, huh? You've probably had her all up in my house, seein' God only knows. All I know is that a young nigga like you has a face like that lookin' up at him from his dick, and he'll say just about anything."

I didn't bother denying that Lauren knew a lot. The fact of the matter was that she did know too much, and even if she didn't, Silas would still want her dead based on the possibility she might. An argument would be futile. Nothing had changed, Silas still wanted her dead. Now even more than he did before.

"And don't think I don't have somethin' for your ass, too, Kain. Caplan's daughter is your girl, I get it. You not tryna have your girl out here unprotected, so it only makes sense that you been blockin' her bounty. I could almost overlook that shit. But that shit with the hit you ruined last spring? Nah, that was wasted time and money. And I ain't raised no rats. If not for you bein' my son, I could smoke you right now for what you done. But I got somethin' else for your ass. Maybe even worse than death."

Above all else, this only made me curious. What could be worse than death? So I asked.

Silas stirred the ice in his cup, taking his time with his response as he downed his final drink. When my father's eyes drew up from the remnants of the brown liquor in his glass, he made me a promise.

"I'm gonna make you watch her die."

Chapter Nine

KAIN

The door to the house in Pembroke Pines was kicked in when I arrived. When I'd stepped in to find the place I'd once called home trashed beyond recognition on the inside, I can't say I was surprised. If Silas had burned the house to the ground, even that would've been a believable outcome. My fingers traced along the dented surfaces of broken furniture, feet stepping around scattered papers along the ground. In the morning, I would be calling two people—a cleaning service and a real estate agent.

Now that Silas knew about this place, keeping his threats in mind, the only thing left to do was sell it. Despite the fact that I'd grown to really like this place, I was not grieving its upcoming sale. The last couple of weeks had really shown me that the appeal of the house had never really been the rooms, but the person in them with me. So when I walked in to find the house had been turned upside down and shook, all I could do was be grateful that Lauren wasn't here while it had happened.

I'd only come back to grab a few dozen clothing items to hold Lauren over for a few days until she might need to get some more things. For now, the two suitcases I'd tucked into the trunk of my car would be enough to hold us both over. The drive back to *The Bayside* would need to have lots of twists and turns and stops—insurance in case Silas was having me followed.

I checked the time on my wrist watch. It was only six o'clock in the evening. No more than ten hours ago, I'd watched my best friend of over fifteen years get lowered into the ground, and before I could even get a chance to grieve, I was steady trying to keep my pulse under control as I worked my ass off to make sure my girl wouldn't suffer the same fate.

In truth, I was stressed as fuck.

All my life, Silas had never really been able to hold anything over my head. With us being from the same family, I had nothing he could take from me. After he'd transferred his billion-dollar crime empire over to me to protect his assets in case of legal setbacks, he'd really thrown the ball in my court. For all intents and purposes, I could do as I pleased with every penny Silas had ever made. Before today, my father trusted me so much that essentially he put himself at my mercy by allowing me to control his money.

I thought I was untouchable.

And as I walked out of my father's office not too long before, I think we both knew I still was. Why else would he have merely yelled at me for doing something we both knew was unforgivable? Silas concluded what I already figured—he couldn't kill me. If not for fatherly love reasons, Silas still couldn't kill me because I had all his money. Unless I transferred it all back, Silas would never be able to murder me without losing everything in the process.

I *was* untouchable.

But *she* wasn't.

After one last go-through of the house, I'd stopped at the landline mounted in the kitchen, pulling out the phone number for Lauren's room from the back pocket of my black dress pants. Still wearing the clothes I'd worn to Amir's funeral, I loosened the black tie around my neck as the phone began to ring.

"Hello."

Even though I knew she'd been safe all along, hearing the sound of her voice did something to release some of the tension I'd been feeling. Lost in my own relief, I'd forgotten to respond and her second hello came out a little more frantic.

"Hey sorry, relax... I'm fine," I tried to calm her down. "You okay?"

"Am *I* okay?" she repeated back to me as if to get me to realize how ridiculous of a question that was. *She right...* "Kain, what happened?"

There was no way I could tell her the whole truth without scaring her half to death, so I danced around the topic. "He was mad, but at the end of the day, there's not much he can do to me without doin' himself in. I stopped by the house and got your clothes. Do you need anything here that you think I might leave behind? It's gonna be a little bit before I get back, but I'll be back tonight."

She sighed on the other end, relieved.

"The only thing there that I need is you."

I cracked a half smile, repeating, "I'll be back tonight."

* * *

I wasn't surprised to find Jay's car parked outside of Marlon's house when I'd pulled into the driveway. My other two close friends had not been present for Amir's funeral this morning, so it only made sense that they were spending the day together, walking down a lane of memories, having their own little at-home funeral for our recently departed group member.

"And then there were three," Jay announced aloud the minute I'd let myself through Marlon's front door. Jay could be particularly crass when he was sober, but as I walked into the scene of tobacco rolling paper and a half-drunk bottle of Hennessy sprawled along the surface of Marlon's living room coffee table, I knew Jay's tasteless remark was a product of any one of those things.

Marlon laid in silence, hands behind his head and eyes closed. If I didn't know him, I would think that he was sleeping, but no, that's just how Marlon rides through his highs.

"You went to the funeral?" Marlon asked, a hitch of surprise in his tone. His eyes weren't open to see my suit, so I was inclined to ask how he knew, but I didn't.

"Yeah, I went."

"I bet you Faye made the ceremony religious as fuck," Marlon guessed.

Faye was Amir's mother, the closest thing I ever had to a mother all my life. She'd taken me under her wing when I was in second grade, and for fifteen years she treated me just like she treated her son. Today, however, I lost her, too.

Although she wasn't angry enough to ask me to leave, she knew there would be no funeral today if not for my friendship with her son. And for that, she treated me accordingly, thanking everyone at the ceremony for coming except for me.

I couldn't be mad at that. She had every right.

"Yeah, it was pretty religious."

"See, that's another reason I wouldn't go," Jay bellowed. "Everybody doing everything they can to keep from dyin' in these streets, but the minute someone dies, black folks steady dancing in church, praising the life lost."

"It wasn't like that," I muttered, taking a seat at the end of the worn, brown couch. Nobody was celebrating Amir's departure. The morning was dark and filled with hateful glares. No one talked about the good times. No one expressed happiness over the possibility that Amir was in the kingdom of heaven. And certainly, no one danced.

Possibly noting the out of character tone in my voice, Marlon opened up one eye before sitting up and opening them both. He bluntly asked, "Where's Button?"

He asked the question in place of asking, '*What's wrong?*'

I didn't know whether to be annoyed at Marlon's concern for Lauren, or to be appreciative of it. I chose neither, deciding to outright ignore his question because if I checked him for it, I'd be doing too much. Marlon was not pining after my girl. He just wanted to make sure she was alright. Lauren just had that effect on people. Even Vance had caught wind of it. But I didn't have the patience for Marlon's intrusiveness right now.

"She's fine," I got straight to it, my delivery a bit short. Marlon's shoulders relaxed and he laid back down after drawing in one long drag from a blunt on the table. Jay poured himself another glass of Henny, offering me a glass after filling his own.

I refused, a small part of me remembering why I was never as close with Marlon or Jay as I was with Amir, why I called Marlon and Jay my friends and Amir my brother.

Amir would have caught on straight away.

Amir would have noticed something was seriously wrong, that I was not okay. And he would've questioned it, not really expecting a straight answer, but at least extending the gesture.

But Amir was dead.

Forever lifeless under six feet of dirt. I'd watched his casket lower into the hole myself, an image I deeply regretted allowing myself to see. I envied the fact that Jay and Marlon didn't have that picture burned into the forefronts of their minds. I envied that they could dull their emotions with alcohol and weed.

Smoking with Vance didn't make the images of that lowering casket go away.

Drinking with Silas didn't do that either.

Going to the funeral was a mistake. Not because of the unwelcoming faces that met my arrival, but because going to the funeral somehow made Amir's death even more real.

And I had no idea how to deal with any of this.

Every light in Sanaa's house was lit when my car pulled in to her driveway. I was still stalling for time, being a little cautious about going straight back to Lauren on the off chance I was being watched. Since leaving Marlon's house, I hadn't really seen any cars or faces that looked familiar. Stopping at Sanaa's was just my attempt at being thorough.

From the looks of the cars out front, my other sister Monique was visiting Sanaa as well. On any other day, the idea of being around the both of them as they fussed and bickered would've had me start the engine of my Camaro right back up. Today, though...

Today was just different.

As always, Sanaa's door was unlocked. At the sound of the front door closing, the chattering I heard coming from the living room came to an abrupt stop. I kept my steps quiet, shaking off the stuffy black suit jacket I had over my white button up, as I moved further into the house.

A sound like shushing rang as I rounded a corner toward the living room, followed by loud and defensive screaming while my older sister, Sanaa, tried to lunge at me with a broom handle. She aimed for my head.

"Sanaa, it's me!" I barely caught the wooden staff in my hand.

"Oh my God, Sanaa, it's just Kain!" Monique called frantically from behind her, rushing to grab at her arms, repeating, "It's just Kain!"

"Kain!" Sanaa screeched, dropping the broom handle on the ground by her side. "Kain, what the fuck is your problem! You scared the shit out of us. Why didn't you just *knock*?"

I huffed out in frustration, annoyed. "Because. You. Never. Lock. Your. Doors."

This was an ongoing issue between my sister and I. She made it so easy to break into her house. I'd muddled over the idea of leaving Lauren at Sanaa's before deciding on *The Bayside*. The one reason I could not leave Lauren with my sister who liked her best was because Sanaa clearly lived in a different universe than the rest of us, a universe that was unrealistically safe. Rarely did she ever operate with caution in anything she did.

"What are you doing here?" Monique asked, a slight hint of suspicion in her tone.

Sanaa read my mind, replying, "Damn, Mo. Kain can't come visit his big sister every once in a while? Why are *you* here? To see me, right? So is Kain."

Ever since the dinner with Lauren, where Monique found out Lauren was the daughter of Joshua Caplan, she had visibly lost a little faith in me. Sanaa, though... Once she decided she liked someone, she liked them. So even though I was sure that time had allowed for Sanaa to get the full run down about who Lauren was and everything that came with that, it didn't stop her from genuinely asking, "How is the girlfriend?"

Behind her, Monique released an uncomfortable sigh.

I understood her discomfort. Dating the daughter of Miami's most crooked prosecutor was really high up there on the list of things I absolutely shouldn't do.

"Oh quit your loud sighing, Monique." Sanaa's head snapped back. "If we were all judged on what our daddies do, then none of us would stand a chance in this world. How's the girlfriend?" she pressed enthusiastically.

I could always count on Sanaa's optimism.

"She's alright." I didn't mention Dad's threat to Lauren's life looming over my head. Actually, I didn't say anything. I had no words, just confusing knots twisting in the pit of my stomach that made me want to be around some people who understood me.

I'd never felt this way before.

Going over Marlon's just didn't cut it. Watching Marlon and Jay deal with their grief with weed and Hennessy just wasn't my coping mechanism, and I wasn't in the mood to join them, either. After that talk with Silas, I wouldn't complain if I had to go without another glass of cognac for at least a few months.

Monique broke the silence, nodding me over to the couches in the living room. "Amir's funeral was this morning. How you holding up, K?"

I could always count on Monique's perceptiveness.

Given the reminder and finally noticing what I was wearing, Sanaa remembered. "Oh right, that *was* today."

I took it neither of them had been told about Cierra's big reveal to Silas earlier. Knowing they'd give her hell for it, I kept to myself. I was pissed as hell at Cierra for what she'd done, but somehow I got the sense that whatever I was feeling about Amir's death was hitting her five times as hard. Knowing how fucked up my emotions were, anything worse than this was sure to drive a person insane.

And that's what Cierra's behavior was today—insanity driven by grief.

"Kain, are you okay?" Monique's voice grew soft as though she was talking to one of her patients.

"Yeah," I replied after a long pause. I don't know why I lied. I could've told the truth, that I wasn't okay at all, and no one would've been surprised. Still, I lied again, "Yeah, I'm fine."

"You know," Sanaa said the words slowly. "When I was in college, my best friend in the whole wide world died in a car accident. I cried for months. I was always picking up my phone to call her at random hours of the day, only to realize I couldn't anymore. It crushed me." Something in my chest twisted. My sister's words were extremely relatable. She had me until she said the words, "I know how you feel."

"Do you?" I asked dismissively. "Who was drivin' the car when your friend died? Was it you?"

"Well no, but—"

"Then you don't know, Sanaa."

"Kain." Monique laid an assuring hand on the back of my shoulder, waiting for me to meet her eyes before she said, "You know we love you, right?"

I nodded, somehow feeling like this exchange only created distance. Something about Monique's words made me feel like I was making my problem everyone's problem, and so I reeled back. I took in a deep breath and checked my watch, deciding now was a safe enough time to head over to The Bayside.

"I gotta go," I announced. My abrupt statement drew confusion out of them, and so I simply lied again. "I was only stoppin' by 'cause I was in the neighborhood."

I shook Monique's hand off my shoulder before rising to my feet, offering my sisters halfhearted smile before beginning my trek to the door. Of course, they followed after me, keen to walk me to my car.

Eager to not end the visit on a depressing note, when I got to my car door, Sanaa asked, "What are you doing for your birthday?"

I shrugged, not caring because it actually hadn't crossed my mind that I was turning twenty-one at the end of July. Clearly I had more pressing matters to think about. Besides, it was still June. This was far from important.

Not according to Sanaa, though. As a professional event planner, she was absolutely appalled I hadn't made plans.

"What?!" She practically shouted. "But it's the 30th of next month! Twenty-one is a party birthday! You can finally drink alcohol." She thought about what she'd just said and amended it, "Well… you can finally drink alcohol *legally*."

"It's really not that deep."

"*Noooooo*." She wasn't having it. "Monique, tell him that twenty-one is a party birthday."

Monique brought up her shoulders, spreading out her arms like she couldn't dispute this. "It's not just *a* party birthday. It's *the* party birthday."

Sanaa's eyes grew wide as she nodded. "Seriously."

I could see where this was going. Sanaa wasn't just trying to get me to celebrate my birthday, she wanted to use this as an opportunity to plan a party with a big budget. It was more for her than for me when I sighed and said, "Do whatever you want, Sanaa."

"You mean it?" She was beaming, and so I had to nod. "Get me Lauren's number. I want her input on this."

Like me, Lauren didn't have a phone right now.

"I'll have to get back to you on that."

"Kain, your birthday is in thirty-five days!" Sanaa stressed as if this wasn't nearly enough time.

Given Sanaa's behavior, I was already beginning to get the sense that this party was gonna be unnecessarily extravagant. If Lauren was in on the planning, at least she'd know to keep this low key. I would be giving Sanaa her number for that reason alone.

"Yeah, I'll get it to you as soon as possible," I promised, in a rush, and reaching for the door handle of my car. Just before I could get inside, Monique stopped me for a moment, eyeing me carefully. I paused, turning to face her worrisome dark eyes.

Her hands came up to meet my shoulders, not letting up on the eye contact when she asked, "And you're sure you're alright?"

Effortlessly... I lied.

"Yeah, Mo," I replied with a nod. "I'm fine."

The door to The Bayside suite had barely cracked six inches before it swung open wider, revealing Lauren to be standing on the other side. At the exact moment that her arms clasped around me, circling my neck in an almost desperately firm hold, the bags in my hands dropped. My hand came around her, both to return her hug, and because it wasn't until her arms were around me that I realized that this—*her*—this was what I'd needed all day.

You would've thought Lauren hadn't seen me in days from the tightness of her grip. Though I didn't mind. On a day when it just felt like everything about me was falling apart, as long as she continued to hold tight, I could keep it together.

It was several seconds before Lauren finally pulled back, her big eyes seemingly scanning every inch of me for out of place hairs. If I so much as got a papercut today, she would find it.

"Are you hurt anywhere?"

"No, I told you I was fine." Like I told everyone else.

"Yeah, but you're the type to lie about that."

A crease formed between my eyebrows, the only hint at my surprise to be read so accurately. I didn't bother lying. Instead I reached back, finally shutting the room door behind me. Even as I slid the luggage I'd brought up out of the way, Lauren had yet to let me go.

Honestly, I didn't want her to.

The therapeutic quality of her vanilla-scented hair always did well to ease something inside me. As I tucked a stray curl behind her ear, Lauren eyed me carefully, her eyes moving along every detail of my face, and somehow I got the feeling that even though I was keeping a perfectly straight expression—she knew.

"Are you okay?" Lauren asked, her tone conveying that even though she was asking, she could already tell what the answer was. My knee-jerk reaction was to lie, but the one-word response stopped at the tip of my tongue, and I could only look at her. Lauren tried to ask me again. "Kain, are you—"

"No." It was an odd mixture of relief and pain that settled at the base of my chest then. Pain because acknowledging the emotions coursing through me almost had an amplifying effect on them, but relieved because, one look at her and I knew I wouldn't have to deal with them on my own. I shook my head in resignation, finally being honest about it out loud. "No, I'm not okay."

Chapter Ten

KAIN

The sound of Lauren's heartbeat kept me anchored to the bed where we laid. With my head set against her chest, the steady rhythm of her beating heart through the fabric of her funeral dress had a calming effect, like a lullaby. Behind me, I could feel her finger tracing soothing circles along the back of my head, the sound of her breathing matching the calmness of her heart.

"What do you feel right now?" she questioned softly.

"I don't know." I really didn't. "Today's just been a lot."

"Start from the beginning then. Tell me about your day."

"Well, the funeral... You were there. That was..."

"Tense," she finished my sentence, finding just the right word.

"I shouldn't have went."

"Did going make you feel worse?"

"It didn't make me feel better."

"Do you think you'll always feel that way?"

I'd never been to any form of therapy before, but I knew a therapy session when I heard one. Lauren was cross examining me, asking me leading questions so that I could find the answers to my own questions from within. I had to smile at her efforts. Knowing that she had goals of becoming a psychiatrist someday, I didn't mind letting her practice on me.

"I probably won't always feel this way." When all these feelings subsided, several years down the line, going to the funeral would likely be one less regret for me. I could see where Lauren was trying to lead. It didn't make me feel better in that moment, but it did give me something to look forward to.

"And so then with your father," she encouraged me to keep talking. Even though talking to Lauren did have its easing effects, I made a decision to keep Silas' threats to myself. As far as she knew, he'd wanted her dead for a while now, so making a point to tell her about his latest threat would only scare her unnecessarily. So I kept the details quiet.

"Nothin' new," I replied. "You just gotta continue to be careful in these streets. But I got you. Trust me?"

"I trust you." She was sincere. "But who's got you, Kain? Who keeps you safe?"

I turned my head in order to meet her eyes, indifference in my voice when I responded, "I keep me safe."

Wordlessly, she nodded, her eyes growing sympathetic. "You look so tired."

"I'll sleep soon." It was a little after midnight, the only light in the room coming in from outside, silvery light from the night sky, giving Lauren's brown skin a cool blue undertone. The full moon reflected back at me against the nearly black irises of her eyes. There was always such warmth in Lauren's eyes. It's how I knew she loved me before she even told me.

I wondered what she saw in mine.

"No." Lauren shook her head. "You don't look sleepy. You look… *tired*."

I didn't know what to say to this. I wasn't even sure I had fully grasped what she was trying to tell me. Without an explanation, Lauren's fingers wrapped around the collar of my white dress shirt, pulling me towards her. Of course I didn't resist.

"You don't have to put up a front for me," she whispered against my lips, pressing her forehead to mine. There was something almost disarming about the gentleness of her words. "You can be vulnerable with me. Kainie, you can cry."

When she pulled back, her soft hands were on either side of my face as said the words, "Let it out."

She waited, but there were no tears. I couldn't do what Lauren was telling me to. It went against everything that I believed myself to be, everything I was told I had to be. It wasn't that I just wouldn't do it.

I honestly didn't know how.

"You're so tired," she whispered, tears readily pooling at the rims of her eyes. I reached in to catch the first one before it could fall. Lauren made crying look easy.

I couldn't remember the last time I shed tears for anything. I supposed that's what mothers are for. They sit you down real calm like and tell you that it's okay to cry if that's what you're feeling at that point in time. I might've had that once upon a time. If I did, I certainly didn't remember.

When it came to my mother, I didn't try to grasp at memories that weren't there. Once upon a time there was a younger version of myself that often wondered where she was, but years of having a front row seat to the depths of my father's ruthlessness told me that wherever she was, she likely had no intentions of coming back. Even if that meant abandoning me.

It was nothing to lose sleep over. You can't miss what you never knew.

But it was in moments like this that I would think of her the most. When your girl looks you square in the eye and tells you that it's okay to cry, only for you to realize you've forgotten how, you think about your mother, you think about how she wouldn't have let you forget.

But it is what it is.

Accepting things as they are and not wasting time mourning them is practical. And I suppose coming to that realization is what fathers are for. I had a lot of that growing up. I could still hear echoes of Silas ringing in my head from when I was just a boy.

It is what it is, Kain. What you cryin' for?

He said these things so often that it wasn't long before I began saying them to myself, hearing his voice in my head any time I might fuck around and feel something.

And then one day, the voice stopped, and everything felt more numb than it did before. Resulting from a constant dulling of my emotions that turned the world around me into metaphorical shades of gray. Life lost all color. And the only time I could get it back was when I saw red. Soon, the only time I really felt anything was when I got angry.

To hear Silas tell it, I became a man.

* * *

Lauren picked at her breakfast, having little to no appetite it seemed. It bothered me today especially because I was sure she hadn't eaten all day yesterday as she waited for me to come back. It had never been like me to give a damn about whether or not people skipped their meals. But Lauren had lost weight in the time between the Poseidon Massacre and now. I suspected that although some of that was on me, I knew something else was weighing heavily on her mind.

"Baby, we need to talk about your family."

Lauren flinched. I guessed right. That was it. She shrugged at first, shaking her head as if to say none of it mattered. I only looked at her, waiting patiently for her to speak.

"While you were in the shower, I turned on the local news," she revealed. "Uh... nothing too major. You know, with the um... With the court proceedings against your father set for August, local reporters stopped by my dad's office and interviewed him about how the investigation was going."

It'd been a little over a week since Lauren had shown up at my doorstep, having been kicked out of her home by her father earlier that day. This news interview she'd watched would've been her first time seeing her father in days.

"He looked..." Her voice cracked. "...normal."

I wasted no time rising from my seat at the table, stopping at her side in a crouch as she remained seated. She turned to face me, hurt still prominent in her voice as she spoke.

"He kicked me out in the middle of the night with no phone and no money, and hasn't heard from me in days. And to see him on the news, complaining about how your family is standing in the way of him securing any witnesses, as if that was the only problem he has right now... I just... It's like he doesn't even care about me, Kain."

I leaned in, tucking a finger under her chin so that she wouldn't look down.

"Can I be honest with you?" I asked.

"Sure." She nodded, wiping away at a tear that had found its way travelling down her cheek. "Go ahead, be honest with me."

"Your Pops..." I sighed, shaking my head in irritation. "Your Pops ain't shit."

If ever there was a way for a laugh to sound sad, it was Lauren's laugh in that moment.

"No, I mean it. It's a well-known fact out here that Joshua Caplan is literally the worst human being in Miami."

"Worse than *your* father?" she hit back.

"Shit, he just *might* be," I replied with a chuckle, taking her by the hand and leading her into the living room for a seat. "Your father is a ruthless piece of shit."

"Well I can see why you would feel that way, considering you come from a crime family."

"Nah," I replied with a shake of my head. "It's not about that at all. Your father is on some next level bullshit with how he operates. He knowingly puts innocent people in prison because he's more concerned with his image and conviction rate over everything. Your father is crooked and egotistical. Trust me, I know what I'm talkin' about. My father's just the same."

"Why are you telling me all of this now?"

"Because parents, at the end of the day, are just people. They have character flaws just like the rest of us. Your father is no different. I don't think you've realized this yet." When she hit me with the confused eyebrows, I tried my best to explain. "Your father is a walking ego, and like all egoists, he will never love anyone as much as he loves himself."

I reached into the distance between us, holding her as I continued to lay the ugly truth at her feet.

"Your father sees your decision to be in a relationship with the likes of me, a Montgomery, as an affront to everything he's worked for—a threat to his image. Lauren, I'm sure your father does love you, but so long he continues to see your decisions as a threat to him and what he's worked for, he will always love himself first. Know that."

"He never used to be like this," she whispered.

"You never used to give him a reason to be."

"Does my father really get innocent people put in prison? How?"

"You'd be surprised to find out just what kind of man he is," I warned. When she didn't back down, I told her a few things I knew. "Your father has a notorious reputation around here. He's not above convicting the wrong person if it means his picture is still put in the paper. He will step on whoever needs to be stepped on. And I know you think my family is threatening the witnesses so that they don't testify against Silas, but... Your father's track record with witnesses is really why he can't find any willing people to take the stand."

"His track record?"

"Yeah, when he manages to get a witness and loses the case, your father does absolutely nothin' to ensure those people are safe on the outside. Once your father doesn't feel like he needs them, he's content to let them die." I shook my head, tone serious when I revealed, "And they always die. That's why nobody wants to take the stand for your father against Silas. Because if Silas doesn't lose, they're as good as dead. Your father won't do anything to help them. And everybody knows it."

"I think I'm going to be sick," Lauren whispered, a nauseous look settling into her features. "Everybody may have known this, but I never did."

"Yeah." I nodded. "That's normal. The ability to see our parents for what they are comes with the ability to see them as people first. Once you do that, the warning signs essentially reveal themselves, but enough about this -- let's get out of here."

This seemed to take her by surprise. "Wait – you mean, like, outside?"

I nodded. "What else would I mean?"

"But aren't you worried about—" She stopped, her eyes widening. It was then that Lauren realized the obvious. Now that Silas knew about us, there was nothing left to keep secret. "Well, what about the local gossip blogs?"

"What about them?"

When she realized she didn't have an answer to that, I could only crack a smile. I didn't care about showing up on Miami gossip sites, and if she didn't, there was no reason for us to stay in this hotel room all day.

"Come on." I nodded for her to follow me to the door. "I need a new phone, and so do you. *Especially* you, actually."

"What do you mean by that?"

"Sanaa asked for your number yesterday," I replied, explaining, "She needs your help with something."

Chapter Eleven

KAIN

In only ten days, there were a total of fourteen local news segments about Lauren and I being sighted in various spots around Miami. To the local media, she wasn't even referred to by name, but as Joshua Caplan's daughter. The son of Miami's biggest crime magnate and the daughter of Miami's district attorney in a relationship—it was an instant scandal.

The attention wasn't too intrusive—people knew to stay out of my way—but Lauren wasn't used to any of it. After one evening in which we got followed back to *The Bayside* by local photographers, we both decided that it would just be safer to stay low key.

Whether or not we cared about the world knowing about us, that didn't change the death threat Lauren had looming over her head. I hadn't anticipated this much buzz. Although I knew the constant eyes on us were definitely making it harder for my father to plot on Lauren, photographers giving away our location to Silas was the straw that broke the camel's back.

We'd immediately checked out of the hotel, and found ourselves in what was probably the safest place we could go.

My sister Sanaa's house, which had been my second choice initially before I picked The Bayside. Now that the hotel was no longer an option—Sanaa it was.

Sanaa lived in an upscale gated community, surrounded by professionals who couldn't care less about who Silas Montgomery's son was dating. Also, I knew that sending anyone to Sanaa's house was definitely a deterrent for my father. No matter how much he wanted Lauren dead, Silas had a policy to never get my sisters involved in his business.

Sanaa didn't take much convincing either. For ten days, she and Lauren had been going back and forth over the phone, planning a birthday party I didn't actually want to have. So when I asked her if it would be alright if Lauren stayed with her, Sanaa was already sold, enthralled by the idea of having her party planning partner in-house.

When it came to my sisters, Sanaa seemed to be the only one supportive of my relationship. On one hand of the spectrum, I had Cierra, who I hadn't heard from since the funeral and probably wouldn't hear from any time soon, and on the other end was Sanaa. Monique fell somewhere in between, not hating Lauren, but certainly not in favor of the idea of my being with her. Petra, my other sister who lived in Memphis, would likely choose whichever position Monique decided to take.

Life could be so complicated sometimes.

I was sitting alone in Sanaa's dining room.

Four days had passed since Lauren and I had checked out of The Bayside, making it a total of two weeks since Amir's funeral. I was just starting to get back into the groove of my LSAT prep coursework, turning through pages of logical reasoning practice questions. Lauren was nowhere to be found, probably off somewhere with Sanaa, shopping on the internet for party supplies.

My days had been quieter since deciding to stay at my sister's. During the day, Lauren would leave me alone so that I could find the focus to study. My LSAT was in September, and even given the events of the past month, I had no intention of rescheduling it. Sanaa did more than enough to keep her occupied.

I was happy that Lauren had managed to find a friend in my sister. Even though I was doing my best, I could never be as cheerful and peppy as Sanaa—even before that summer. Sanaa was next level, like a happy virus, spreading smiles and laughs with her jovial energy. She made Lauren smile. And that made me smile.

The sounds of Sanaa's laugh cut through the silence of her dining room, snapping me out of my own head. Lauren was close by as well, her laugh sounding off just as loud.

"Kain, take a study break," my sister encouraged, reaching for the book I had open in front of me. "It's lunch time, and I wanna have it at the table."

Even though I probably shouldn't have, I welcomed the distraction, tossing a glance over at Lauren. Her hair was tied back, away from the sides of her face for a change. She wore an oversized shirt under a pair of overalls, a style I never once thought was attractive until I'd seen her in it. I didn't even realize I was smiling until she returned it, her dimples sinking into her cheeks the way they usually did when her smiles were genuine.

She was happy today.

"Something happen?" I asked curiously.

"Yes!" She was quick to share. "Guess what!"

"What?"

"Sanaa told me she has a family album hidden away somewhere," Lauren beamed.

"Yep," Sanaa nodded. "I just need to find it. Lauren, could you be a doll and get the food out of the fridge while I look?"

"Of course."

"Wait." I reminded them I was still here. "Family album?"

"Yes, Kain," Sanaa huffed. "You know, a book of pictures."

"Yeah, I *know* what a family album is." My sister rolled her eyes, only half listening as she rummaged through the shelves of a storage closet. "But why?"

"Because I told Lauren you were a cute baby and she wants to see."

"Yeah, I want to see," she echoed from the fridge.

I pinched the skin between my eyes, releasing a slow breath. No, I didn't want to spend my lunch looking at embarrassing pictures of me from when I was young. But as Lauren bounced back and forth on the balls of her feet, literally shaking with anticipation over just a few photos, I couldn't help but crack a smile.

If this was the worst thing that could happen while living at Sanaa's, then I considered myself pretty lucky.

* * *

Lauren decided to save a photo of me at age two as the background of her cell phone screen. Every five minutes she would pick up her phone and gush over how—

"This is literally the cutest picture ever." She was doing it again. I turned to give her a look, not quite annoyed, but not quite enthusiastic either. We were sitting up, side by side and sharing a bed in Sanaa's guest room. It was late. Night time seemed to be the only time we were ever together lately. "Look at your little hands! Oh my God, I could literally just eat you up."

"Okay, I get it." I reached for the phone in her hand, setting it aside out of her reach. "I was cute, I get it."

She raised a hand to my cheek, her tone mockingly reassuring when she promised, "Oh, you're still cute, don't worry."

"Hmm," I thought about this, coming in closer as her hand remained on my face. The distance between us gradually shrunk, her lips pressing on to mine gently at first. Against her lips, I replied, "You not too bad either."

She came in for another, her soft lips molding against mine with a precision that often had me feeling like, all this time, Lauren was custom built just for me.

Each subsequent kiss grew longer and deeper than the last, a feverish heat rising between the both of us.

In the days following Amir's funeral—which objectively was the worst day of my life for the fact that I watched my best friend buried, and because of the events that followed immediately after—I found myself happiest in the moments when I could just get lost in her. Lauren had a way of allowing me to forget about the dozens of things stressing me out at any given moment. She cleared out all the noise, and put me at ease.

"Kain," she whispered harshly in the low light of the room, as my hand traveled under the oversized shirt she wore. A rejection was coming. "Kain, we can't."

"Because?" I questioned softly. My hands didn't stop, and she didn't protest as I pulled the shirt over her head, leaving her there in just her panties. Since checking out of *The Bayside*, it had been days since I had her, and Lauren was like a drug—addictive. Going for so long without her was just not fair.

Even as she tried to get me to stop, her lips were still compliant, meeting mine with a desire that didn't match her protests. I smiled against her, traveling lower along her neck, and waiting for the relaxed sounds of her breathing to shift.

"Because," she tried to sound assertive, but the word came out sounding vaguely like a moan. "Because your sister's sleeping next door."

"Mm-hmm," I acknowledged this, moving lower along the skin of her shoulders, tasting her with each bite I left behind. Lauren's mouth was saying we couldn't, but the way she leaned into my touch said otherwise. "And?"

"And we just…" Lauren drew in a sharp breath just as my fingers slipped under the cotton of her panties. She was so wet. "Mm—we just can't."

"Just tell me when to stop."

She didn't say the word.

"Kain," she whispered, completely oblivious about how the breathy quality of her voice was only encouraging me. "You know I'm a…" I slipped two fingers in her, mindful to pay extra attention to her clit with my thumb. Lauren brought her hand up to her mouth, desperate to muffle the sounds of her pleasure in the dead silence of Sanaa's house. "Kain, you know I'm a screamer."

I glanced away from the view of her hardening nipples, meeting her eyes when I replied, "Yeah… I do."

"She's gonna hear us," Lauren protested, barely sounding like she cared at this point.

"Yeah… she might."

"Kain," Lauren whispered my name just as I decided to resume what I was initially doing. And then she said the word. "No."

It was a meek and indecisive *no*, but it was a *no* nonetheless. The first night Lauren and I met, she was in a daunting place, caught between a bed and a rapist. Because of that, if she ever said *no* to me, no matter how unconvincing it was, I would stop.

My hand slipped out of her underwear, and my eyes came back to hers. I was disappointed, but I was smart enough to know not to show it.

"Are you hard?" she asked curiously.

I had to laugh at this. "Are you kidding?"

"Hmm," she considered this, eyes falling to the tent in my pants. "Sorry about that."

There was nothing sorry about the accomplished smile on her face. She was clearly proud of herself. Never in a million years did I ever think I would someday find this kind of teasing ass behavior cute.

"I just make too much noise," she tried to plead her case, tilting her head to the side with eyes that asked me to understand. I simply nodded, trying to respect her choices. "But *you* don't"

"I don't what?"

"You don't make as much noise as I do." Before I could ask, I quickly understood what she was trying to imply. Lauren's hands latched onto the waistband of my pajama pants, a coy half smile turning up her left cheek before she announced, "There's a first time for everything."

Fuck.

Understanding what was going through her mind, my dying erection only took a fraction of a second to come alive again. Lauren took me into her hands, her tongue slowly running along the skin of her lower lip before she nervously bit down.

"Yeah," she whispered more to herself than to me. "So cute I could just eat you up."

In spite of myself, I chuckled.

Lauren could be so corny.

Chapter Twelve

KAIN

The last venue I expected Lauren and Sanaa to hold my twenty-first birthday party was at a strip club. Well, no... Sanaa, I expected this kind of shit from. But Lauren? I would've lost money if I bet on this.

More than thirty days had come and gone so fast. Lauren was still a picture of happiness and health, safe from the clutches of my father even as his court date drew closer and closer. It was July 30th, 2016, thirteen days away from Silas' first day in court. In his last few days leading up to the trial, Silas decided to pay a visit home, back to Memphis. I only knew this because Vance had told me. The last time I'd spoken to Silas was the afternoon after Amir's funeral.

It was a little strange that Silas would want to head to Memphis as if he were making a last ditch farewell to freedom. If I didn't know any better myself, I would say that he had no confidence in his ability to beat this case. It made me curious enough to wonder, but not curious enough to ask.

The Diamond Palace was a family-owned gentleman's club right off I-95, midway between the beach and Downtown Miami. When Lauren pulled the car into park, my first guess was that she was lost. But when she smiled to herself and killed the engine, I pushed out a frustrated sigh. Something about owning dozens of strip clubs definitely takes away some of the appeal.

"Seriously?"

Lauren nodded. "You only turn twenty-one once! Come on, you might actually have fun!"

I doubted it. As a Montgomery, when it came to places like this, I'd seen just about all there was to see, but I didn't say so.

The club was closed off to its regular patrons, affixed with two bouncers at the door with clipboards in their hands. I didn't know who was on the guest list, but I could already guess it'd be the usual suspects—friends from upstate that I made at FSU, Jay and Marlon definitely, and likely a set of people I would have to pretend I remembered the names of. Without checking the list, the bouncers nodded us in.

It's not that I hated parties, I just had to be in the mood for them.

Not too long before this night, Lauren had taken the liberty of diagnosing me with depression. I neither agreed nor disagreed, but it was in moments like this, when the energy all around me was on ten, and I could barely muster a five, that I figured that Lauren might've been on to something.

Walking by my side, the time we'd spent together had definitely been better for Lauren's health. The weight she'd lost from the shit I'd put her through appeared to have come back with a little extra, a view I could appreciate from the way she filled out the tight white dress she had on.

"Lauren!"

The sound of a shrill voice calling out Lauren's name above the music was the first thing to catch my attention. Absently, I could see that the club had been cleaned up quite a bit for the purpose of the party. The usual smell of cheap perfume and lit cigarettes was nowhere to be found. The furniture looked new, which I knew had to have been something Sanaa arranged. Only she was a big enough control freak to think to switch out the lounge seating. *This might be a strip club, but it doesn't need to smell like one*, I could almost hear her saying in my mind.

"Lux!" Lauren called out just as enthusiastically, letting go of my hand. Ahh, I'd heard that name before. It didn't take much investigating to figure that Lauren didn't have that many girlfriends. When she did talk about her friends, however, the name that constantly came up was that of her best friend Lux.

Until (*today*, I guess) recently, Lux had been out of the country for the summer. Seeing how today was the first time in days that Lauren was out and about in public, I could sense an emotional reunion coming. I was five seconds away from excusing myself for a drink when Lauren's hand stopped at my wrist, her eyes shifting ahead as she said to me, "I want to introduce you to my best friend."

So I stayed, doing my best to not look as unenthused as I felt.

Lauren's friend had distrustful eyes. As someone who spent the better half of twenty years under the suspicious gaze of outsiders, I knew that look as soon as I saw it.

"Lux," she introduced herself in one swift syllable, extending a hand for me to shake. Her speech was tight, as was her grip on my hand. It wasn't my style to firmly shake a woman's hand the way I would a man, so her tight clutch was completely one-sided. Still, she didn't weaken her grip, an almost silent threat in the gesture. I didn't know whether to laugh or to feel annoyed.

This girl doesn't like me.

"Kain." I matched her energy. For some reason, Lauren only seemed to pick up on *my* tone, her eyes bouncing between her friend and I.

"Happy birthday, Mr. Montgomery," Lux offered in the exact same fashion I would expect my accountant to wish me a happy birthday. It was formal, cold. *Tense.*

"Mr. Montgomery," I repeated, something I only did when I felt like people couldn't hear themselves. I'd made my decision, choosing to laugh instead of getting annoyed. With a nod of my head, I let her win whatever standoff she thought we were having. "Thanks."

Just before the awkwardness could settle, I wasted no time seizing my chance to bow out for a moment.

"Baby, I'm gonna go get a drink. Can I get you something while I'm over there?"

Something about my question made Lauren both cringe and then smile. "Remember when you taught me how to take shots?"

I chuckled, remembering that evening of course. It was the night we first met. Lauren was the lightest of lightweights.

She shook her head, laughing a little as she declined, "I'm good, thanks. No alcohol for me."

Headed for the bar, just as I walked out of earshot, I could hear Lauren check her friend over the sound of the music. "Lux, what the hell was that all about?"

"Youngblood!"

After getting birthday wishes from about a dozen people I honestly didn't fuck with like that, the sound of my uncle Vance's voice was actually a welcomed one for a change. I was behind the bar, making my own drink. The bartender on duty was a glittery-eyed blonde who looked entirely way too happy to be working this party. Something about her not-so-discrete selfie taking just didn't inspire confidence in her ability to make my order right.

So I was making it myself.

"Woo, you just turned twenty-one and you already mixin' your own drinks? You either a fast learner or you been breakin' the law all this time."

"Funny." I shook the cocktail shaker six times before pouring the mixture into two glasses. They were both supposed to be for me, but now that Vance was here...

Out of necessity, I looked over to where I'd seen Lauren last, making sure she was still sitting with her friend. Sanaa was the type of person to leave her doors open at night, so even though she swore she hired security, I could never be too careful.

Vance followed my gaze and upon getting a look at what I saw, he sighed. There was disappointment in there somewhere.

"You have got it so bad for that one."

"Yeah," I agreed, taking a drink, eyes still on Lauren as she talked with the biggest smile on her face to her friend. Briefly, she glanced my way, eyes catching mine at the bar for a moment, and her smile somehow got even bigger. "I really do."

"You ever think about this long term?"

"I think about a lot of things."

"Seriously, Kain." Vance shook his head, and waited for me to look his way. "Girls like that... They want normal lives. They have dreams of raisin' families behind white picket fences. Thanksgiving dinners with parents, cousins, the whole nine. Regular shit. The things they want the most are essentially the things you will never be able to give."

I took another drink, slamming the empty glass down on the counter. "I know, Vance."

"I don't think you do."

"But I do."

"Then you know that someday, this girl is gonna make you choose."

"I know."

"You say that like someone who has already made a decision." This conversation was giving me déjà vu.

Somehow I got the sense that if Amir was still alive, he would be the one saying these things to me right now. I cringed at the memory of him. Seven weeks later and the wounds were still fresh. Noting that Vance hadn't touched his drink, I reached for it. It disturbed me just a little, seeing the way tossing the drink down in one go helped me cope. *This is how drinking problems start.* "You already chose. You've already made up your mind.," Vance concluded in my silence.

I set the glass down, nodding a confirmation. "Yeah, a while ago actually."

Almost five months ago, after Silas learned of the failed hit on Joshua Caplan, one of his lackeys proposed an easier target.

"We're just now learning that Joshua Caplan has a daughter," Silas was told in the living room the morning that Lauren had decided to stop by her father's office. I was lounging around in the living room, half watching something on TV, phone in my hand. It wasn't long before Silas was sold on the idea of kidnapping and killing her in an effort to fuck with Caplan's ability to focus on his investigation.

I had a decision to make then. I could've turned the other way and let niggas do what they do. Lauren was a short lived person in my life, and if Silas killed her, it would've sucked, but it wouldn't have crushed me. I'd get over it. For all intents and purposes, it should have been an easy decision to make.

It was Lauren or me. Because I just knew choosing Lauren was going to seriously complicate my life.

And even still... Even knowing what I'd be up against if I decided to protect her...

I still chose her.

And knowing what I knew now—knowing what I would lose, knowing *who* I would lose—if I could go back and change my mind...

I poured another drink because of the thoughts in my head. I felt like shit because of the thoughts in my head. The thoughts in my head had me feeling like shit for weeks. Because if I was being completely honest with myself—Amir was dead because I chose her.

And given the opportunity to go back, I knew exactly what I would do. As guilty as it made me feel, there wasn't a doubt in my mind that I knew. I often revisited that day in March, when Silas decided that Lauren was his target, when just before calling Lauren to tell her, I called Marlon, Jay, *and* Amir.

I understood that my actions that day would go on to set the trajectory for the events that would ultimately get Amir killed. I understood the consequences of my actions.

Understanding all of this, if given the chance to go back and change that one decision, I *still* wouldn't change a thing.

And with that, I took another shot.

Chapter Thirteen

KAIN

"Your girl really planned you a party at a strip club. Shit, I underestimated Overalls."

I was buzzed, not drunk, which meant I only had so much patience for Jay right now.

"Yo, she doesn't like that nickname." Jay had taken to calling Lauren Overalls since day one. When he'd met her for the first time she was dressed comfortably, and he seemed unwilling to let her forget it. "Cut that shit out."

Marlon cut some of the tension, leaning forward against the bar counter and observed, "Why'd you let her throw you a party when you know you didn't want one?"

"It was a reason for her to spend some time with my sister."

You could say that it was important to me that at least one of my sisters was on my side about this. Sanaa had planned this party with Lauren for a month straight, obsessing over little things like color schemes, becoming her friend in the process. They'd bonded.

If not for the fact that Lauren's best friend was in attendance, I was sure that she would've been off somewhere with Sanaa, who was probably walking around somewhere with a clipboard, treating this party as if it for one of her clients.

Marlon was saying something I couldn't hear, so rather than ask him to repeat it, I only shrugged, saying nothing and glancing Lauren's way for what was definitely the hundredth time that night. She was still chatting it up with her friend. Evidently Lauren and Lux had a lot of catching up to do.

It was a little after one in the morning, and the party did seem like it was beginning to lose some of its steam. After Vance had called it a night, I'd spent the better part of the evening with my friends, as none of us were really impressed by pole acrobatics anymore.

Like I said, clubs like this lose all of their enchanting flair after some time. And after a lifetime of being at the head of an empire that focused on erecting clubs like this, places like *The Diamond Palace* went from enchanting to strictly business.

Also—and I was sure that Sanaa just didn't know when she chose it—*The Diamond Palace* was one of Lyle's spots back when he was alive. Being here made me feel like his ghost was creeping somewhere, hovering above my neck.

"Amir would have been all the way turnt at this one." Jay meant no harm, but I didn't appreciate the reminder. And it wasn't the first time he'd brought him up this evening. I understood that some people worked through their grief by constantly talking about the person who died, constantly reminiscing.

That wasn't me.

When I found my eyes wandering back to Lauren and her friend yet again, it would've been an understatement to say that I was pleased to see Lux hugging her as if to say goodbye. Over her friend's shoulder, Lauren's eyes found mine, a knowing smile bringing out her dimples.

"*Yeahhhhh*," the word was long and drawn out once I turned my attention back to Marlon and Jay. "I'mma catch you guys later."

* * *

"You never came back to join us." Lauren patted at my shoulder the minute it was within reach.

"Trust me," I expressed, placing a hand at her hip to pull her in closer. "She didn't want me to."

"Right." Lauren frowned. "About that..."

"You can't win over everybody."

"She's not usually that rude."

I cracked a smile. "That... *kinda* makes it worse. Do you wanna get out of here?"

Lauren eyed me, her eyelids drooping ever so slightly as she narrowed her vision.

"You're not having fun," she finally concluded, as if the answers were in my eyes.

"You're the one who diagnosed me with depression," I reminded, as if to say, *'Are you really all that surprised?'*

"Before we go back to your sister's, can we stay a little longer?" she asked.

I looked around the club, knowing full well I didn't want to stay a little longer. Technically, it wasn't even my birthday anymore.

"Not here," Lauren added, grabbing my hand and nodding for me to follow her. It was a trek across the club before she finally came to a stop and nodded toward a threshold behind her. "In here."

Behind Lauren was an opening into a private room, closed off from the rest of the club by a thick velvet curtain. During regular business hours, I knew this closed off space was one of the club's Champagne Rooms, where high paying customers could pay dancers for extra special attention.

Lauren lead the way through the empty and dimly lit space. Under the pink fluorescent lights, Lauren's white dress could almost pass off as rosy, the usual brown of her skin shining red under the colored bulbs. She turned to face me, stopping at a long red chaise, nodding for me to take a seat on it while she stood.

"I saw you watching me from across the room all night."

I took a seat, deciding to play along with whatever she was trying to start. "I wasn't tryna to hide it."

"Do you wanna play a game with me?"

"Depends. What're the rules?"

Lauren pulled up a chair opting to sit across from me. "I'm gonna call it strip therapy."

I chuckled, suddenly becoming all too aware that the red chaise I was on looked like something straight out of a therapist's office. "You can't be serious."

"I am," she asserted. "Lay down, and I'll tell you the rules."

"Lauren."

"Kain," she mocked my tone, encouraging, "Lay down."

Lying down, I asked, "What're the rules?"

"We are going to have a therapy session. For every question of mine that you answer honestly, I will take something off. For every question that you avoid, you will take something off. Easy enough?"

"Yup," I nodded, chuckling to myself before I added, "Now take something off."

"Wait—that question didn't count."

"These are your rules, Lauren. That was a question; I answered."

Rolling her eyes, she leaned backward in her seat, reaching for the back of her white heels.

"Shoes count?"

"I'm wearing a dress. You're wearing a shirt and pants. Let's keep it fair and say I can do one shoe at a time." She waited to see if I would disagree. When I didn't, she reminded, "Also you asked me a question."

"Remember, you didn't say I had to take something off for askin' questions, only avoiding them. These are *your* rules, Lauren." She crossed her arms, visibly annoyed that I was right. "Petty looks cute on you."

"Let's get started then," she urged, thinking for a while before asking her first question. I could tell from the amount of time she took that it was going to be an intrusive one. "What happened that night when you got to Poseidon?"

Sitting up from my laid position, I reached down to unlace both of my shoes, removing both and leaving the socks. "Pass."

"What happened after Poseidon?"

Images of me in Memphis, raising a gun between my aunt Rochelle's eyes, flashed in my memory. Without a word, I removed the socks, too. "Pass."

"If I never showed up at your doorstep with those two men, would you have ever sought me out?"

"Yeah, I just needed some time."

"For?"

"To heal."

"You still haven't healed, though," she observed, and I confirmed this. "You would've shut me out for more than a month."

"It's possible."

"Why?"

"After Amir died, I sort of got it in my head that it only hit me so hard because I'd given him too much of a presence in my day to day life. I thought if I'd kept him at an arm's length, I wouldn't have suffered as much. Distance—I decided—is protective. The further you keep someone away from you, the less affected you will be when they're gone."

"And so you wanted to push me away in case I die or something."

I shook my head at this assumption. "Death isn't the only thing that separates two people. Lauren, I just thought it was best if I didn't *need* you. And when all that shit went down... there was no one else in the world that I needed more. That scared the fuck out of me. Because then I got the strongest sense that everything I was feeling could happen to me all over again, but worse, because next time it would be you."

"What would you do if you lost me?"

I cringed. "I... I don't know, Lauren."

"Are you avoiding the question?"

"No, I *really* don't know," I stressed, reminding her, "You've asked a lot of questions."

"Do you know how many exactly?"

I cracked a smile, knowing it was more than enough for her to be naked right now. "Let's just say it was two."

Nodding, Lauren removed her other shoe and reached for the hem of her dress. With her sitting there in nothing but a sheer black bra and panty combo, I got a feeling that these questions were about to get a lot harder.

"It sounds to me like you fear getting hurt," she figured.

"Doesn't everybody?

"Not this way."

"Explain."

"I don't think you've ever been properly taught how to cope with trauma. You suppress. The things you can't suppress, you avoid. And the things you can't avoid, they eat at you until you deteriorate. And because you know this, you try to protect yourself by keeping your distance. By never allowing yourself to want things, to hope for things, to love anything. Because you wouldn't know what to do if you lost them. You would break."

All I could do was think about her words for a moment, leaning forward in my seat, my elbows resting not far off from my knees.

Lauren wasn't completely wrong.

"That sounds almost spot on. So what do you recommend, Dr. Caplan?"

"Well," Lauren said the word slowly, rising from where she sat and taking a seat beside me. "I recommend you see a real doctor. And get real therapy."

"I'll consider it." I reached in, running my thumb along her cheek. Under the rosy light of the private room, everything about her appeared to come in various shades of pink and red. Lauren and the color red was always such a breathtaking combination. Just before I leaned in to kiss her, she stopped me.

"We're still playing," she informed.

"Ask your two questions then," I whispered, having every intention of answering them in exchange for the last two items she had on.

"This is one question... Why did you say I was almost spot on? What did I get wrong?"

Thumb still caressing her cheek, I replied, "You said I wouldn't allow myself to want things, to hope for things, to love something. That's not all the way true. I've allowed myself to do all of those things."

The vulnerable place it put me in was more stressful than Lauren could ever understand, but I allowed it anyway. I didn't sleep at all the night I realized I loved her. That was the night she was brought to Silas' house by the two men I killed, the same night I'd watched her sleep peacefully in my arms. I knew then, and accepting it was terrifying.

Holding my eyes to hers, Lauren removed her bra.

"Ask your last question."

Rather than speak, Lauren crossed over me, seating herself on my lap, one knee on either side my legs. My hands found their way to her waist, as they always did whenever she straddled me, and she took my face into her hands. Her voice wasn't as confident as before when she whispered her final question.

"Do you love me?"

Against her lips, I quietly confessed, "I do."

If ever there was a way for time to both speed up and slow down within the same period, it happened in that moment. At the exact second that our lips touched, her hands traveled down each and every button of my shirt with an almost lightning fast quickness. Her lips against mine were slow, however, her tongue tasting like Sprite of all things. At this, I smiled into the kiss. Leave it to Lauren to drink Sprite at a party in a strip club.

She wasted no time helping me get just as naked as she already was, wasted no time taking hold of my erection in her palm, and seemed to go too fast to realize we didn't have protection. My hands gripped her waist, holding her still until she raised a look my way.

"Baby, I'm not wearing a—"

"I know," she interrupted with a whisper, her front teeth sinking into the skin of her lower lip nervously before bluntly expressing, "It doesn't matter."

Again, her lips were on mine again, disarming me into loosening my grip at her waist. In a way that was both slow and fast, without hesitation, Lauren lowered herself back onto my lap, taking every inch of me into the tight warmth of her body. When her mouth pushed back, breaking the kiss prematurely, her forehead was still on mine, and she softly said the words, "I love you, too."

* * *

The club was long empty by the time Lauren and I had finally found our way out of the champagne room. She walked barefooted, slightly in front of me, her white heels in one hand and small purse in the other. It was a little after four o'clock in the morning, but Lauren's languid steps were not out of sleepiness at all.

"You need me to carry you?" I offered, a vague sense of accomplishment in my question.

She met my smile with an over exaggerated roll of her eyes. "You're feeling yourself."

"I'm just tryna help," I chuckled, tugging at one of her stray curls teasingly. "But I won't mind watchin' you wobble your way to the car at all."

A half step ahead, she turned to face me, stopping at the club's exit. My eyes rose to find her eyebrows coming together with skepticism.

"Oh, please. I'm not wobbly. We both know you're back there staring at my ass."

"That, too," I agreed, pulling back the door and waiting for her to walk outside. "You wanna get to bed, or are you up for one more stop?"

"A stop where?"

"All I did last night was drink," I explained, coming up behind her as she took steps that definitely *were* wobbly to the car. "I'm starving."

Lauren turned to respond, catching my smirk behind her at the sight of her less than stable steps. "Okay, that's it. Yes, I might be having a little trouble finding my balance. I can't have you standing behind me, stroking your ego over the fact."

"A little trouble finding your balance," I repeated with a chuckle, only laughing harder when she scurried up behind me, no longer wanting me to have the backend view. I turned to look at her, amusement in my voice when I stressed, "Lauren, quit playing games, I need you where I can see you."

I stepped out of the way, nodding for her to walk ahead.

At the exact moment I stepped out from in front of her, a sound like thunder ripped through the early morning silence. Instinctively, my heart fell. Perhaps if I had come from a more run-of-the-mill background, I might've been able to trick myself into believing the sound was thunder at first.

But naturally, unlike thunder, I already knew that close range gunshots would always make my ears ring.

Chapter Fourteen

KAIN

I didn't see who. I didn't see from where. I hadn't seen anything. All I could do was hear *it*, followed by the ringing in my ears.

Hoping to find something, I looked down at my body, searching for injury. I wasn't hurt anywhere. *Fuck*, I'd never wished for physical pain as desperately as I did in that moment.

But damn it, I was *fine*. No gunshot wounds to speak of. *This is not happening*.

Reluctantly, my eyes drew up, not wanting to find what logic ultimately said I would. *If the bullet didn't hit me…*

"Kain." I don't think I'd ever heard her voice sound that way before—a terrifying hybrid of scared and weak. Her hand clutched at her ribcage, just below her left side breast, and underneath her fingers, a growing red stain spread along the white fabric of her dress. "Ka…"

From below, her legs buckled, and if not for my arm reaching out to catch her, she would have fallen face first. *This is not happening…*

But it was.

Internally, my emotions hit so hard they must've knocked the wind out of me. I was on the ground before I knew it, my arm wrapped around her weakening frame. Her free hand came up, clutching tightly at my upper arm. The way her nails dug into my skin confirmed without a doubt in my mind that she was in pain.

But it also told me that there was fight left in her.

"Lauren," my words were automatic, my brain seemingly running on some adrenaline powered autopilot. I didn't even recognize my own voice. Lauren's grip on the fabric of her dress where the blood stain was spreading was tight, but she wasn't applying any pressure. She was bleeding out. "Lauren, baby, move your hand, I need to apply pressure to the… Baby, *please* move your hand."

The warmth of her blood running through my fingers only seemed to send a chill running straight through me. I pressed my palm firmly against her, willing the stream of red to stop if not at least slow down. With my other hand, I reached for the purse that she'd dropped, and for the first time in my life, I dialed 9-1-1.

They took forever.

The whole left side of Lauren's white dress was painted red, a horrifying puddle of blood collecting under her. I tried not to look, opting to focus on the gentle rise and fall of her chest, trying to not to dwell on the fact that as the minutes passed, each rise and fall grew shallower than the last.

"I need you to hold on to the sound of my voice, Lauren. Just listen and breathe." Her grip on my upper arm had long grown limp, and now the only thing I had left in order to confirm that she was still with me were the barely-there breaths she took in abnormal intervals. "I'm so sorry for the last couple of weeks. I understand that I was sulky, and hard to be around for most of the time we were together. I'm sorry if I made you feel helpless, like there was nothing you could do. I should have told you that just you being there made every day easier to get through."

The backs of my eyes stung like pins and needles, and it wasn't until the first couple of clear drops fell, mixing in with her blood around me, that I realized what that was. Lauren always seemed to make crying look easy. What she'd neglected to mention was how fucking painful it was.

"Baby, I'm so sorry." My voice cracked, faltering under the waterfall of emotions hitting me at once. I was apologizing for everything now. "I'm sorry for telling you I didn't care the first time you said you loved me. I'm so sorry I didn't come back for you after *Poseidon*. I'm sorry I didn't tell you I loved you sooner."

It was as if she was taking one breath per minute now. The paramedics I'd called at least a half hour earlier were nowhere to be seen, and I was starting to panic.

"Please hold on to the sound of my voice. I'm right here with you. I love you, and I'm right here with you."

Real life ain't a movie. The world don't stop just because you love somebody.

I counted to one hundred and four in my mind, on the edge of sanity as I waited for a sign that she was still breathing. If she was, I could no longer tell. Not a moment too soon, the sounds of sirens finally rang through the air.

But it was too late.

She wasn't breathing.

And with that realization, everything went numb. I was hardly aware of the arms that pulled me back and away from her until she was roughly snatched out of my hands. Medics with the words *Jackson Memorial* scrawled across their backs surrounded her lifeless body, shouting at one another like they had no sense of cohesiveness.

"I don't believe she's breathing!"

Somehow, overhearing what I already knew confirmed seemed to hit me like a new wave of agony. I wiped at my eyes in an effort to clear my vision, only to remember with horror that my hands were covered in her blood.

"Get me a pair of scissors, and fire up the AED."

They cut through the front of her dress, sticking a wired patch on her upper chest another at her side.

"Do I have a charge? Okay, a hundred and twenty volts! Clear!"

A sound like static rang through the air.

"One thirty! Clear!"

Nothing.

"One more time, one thirty! Clear!" An audible beep sounded off once. "A pulse. We've got a pulse."

* * *

I was held for a total of six hours by Miami-Dade PD. After being kept in a room for five and a half hours, my clothes still drenched in the blood of my girlfriend, when they finally did get around to questioning, I kept silent out of habit. They wanted to know what I saw, what I heard, all of that. It wasn't my first time being questioned by law enforcement, and even though I wanted the person behind all of this to be punished, talking to the police was never an option.

"I don't know," I must've said for the eightieth time, though this particular question I really didn't know the answer to. Having no charges to hold me for, I was inevitably released.

Rather than waste time going home for a change of clothes, I stopped at a pharmacy across the street from Jackson Memorial Hospital and bought myself a generic black hoodie. The blood stains against the black fabric of my pants were barely visible, and so I didn't bother doing anything when it came to those. Although unseen, the nurse's station at Jackson Memorial could clearly still smell the blood on my clothes when I walked up to the reception desk.

"Is Dr. Montgomery-Bryce on duty today?"

My sister Monique was a trauma surgeon at Jackson Memorial. I had no hope of getting any of Lauren's information out of anyone in this hospital but her.

"We're sorry, Dr. Montgomery-Bryce is in surgery."

"Do you know when she's going to be *out* of surgery? This is a fuckin' emergency." A few overhearing nurses turned their heads at the forcefulness of my voice.

"Sir, you're in an emergency room. Everyone is having an emergency."

"Fuck it, I'll just wait in her office." I jumped over the barrier, headed in the direction where I knew Monique's office would be.

"Sir, you can't just—"

"Elise, let it go," I heard another voice interrupt behind me as I continued to walk on. "That's Monique's younger brother."

The outside door to Monique's office was locked, and after knocking rather loudly, it was confirmed that Monique must've still been in surgery. I found a place to sit near a seating area with a water cooler and fake plants.

My thoughts were racing, a back and forth tennis game of emotions in which I was expecting the worst and desperately hoping for the best. Back and forth, back and forth, unable to sit, just pacing back and forth, up and down the halls outside of Monique's office. When an hour had passed with no sign of my sister, I looked overhead at the hospital signs for directions, making a decision to wait for her outside of the operating room she was working in.

Passing through the sterile corridors of Jackson Memorial, a familiar face jumped out at me midstep. For the briefest second, I felt happy, relieved. Only for my eyes to later pick up on the differences that let me know I was not looking at Lauren. What a cruel ass way to be reminded she had an identical twin sister.

Morgan.

I saw her before she saw me, but when her eyes did raise, her expression darkened. It was as if she were looking in the eyes of her sister's shooter. I knew that look because Amir's mother had given me one just like it. Morgan sat on the floor, her head leaning back against a wall tiredly. Her eyes were pink from crying no doubt, and on her upper left arm, thick white gauze bandages were wrapped around. As if she'd very recently given blood, I noted, coming to the conclusion that she'd probably just did. Lauren had lost so much.

I didn't have any other options.

So I spoke to her.

"Is she—"

"*Don't*," Morgan whispered, raising a hand to stop me. "I'm not naïve like Lauren. Don't stand there and act like you care about her, because I don't buy it."

Something in my chest twisted, and I realized that even though Lauren's sister couldn't have been more wrong, I didn't have the energy or desire to fight her on this. It felt like time was slipping through my fingers, and I didn't have enough of it to argue. I didn't even want to. It could've been because I was tired, it could've been because of the disarming effect Morgan's resemblance to her had on me.

"At least tell me if she's alive."

Morgan scoffed. "Last I checked, barely."

"Do you know what room she—"

"I wouldn't tell you even if I knew."

And so I walked on, deciding I would get the answers without her help. It wasn't until I'd arrived outside of the surgery wing that a hospital employee finally questioned my aimless walking around. I tried to ignore them, but that only made them get loud.

"Sir, do you need help?"

The sound of their voice only drew attention my way, turning curious heads. Among them, a familiar face. I'd only ever met Joshua Caplan in person once. It was an evening after I had a date with Lauren, and he tried to punch me in the face. For Lauren's sake, I had let it go.

"No," I replied to the short statured security guard beside me. "I don't need help. I'm just waiting on a family member."

"What the hell is he doing here?"

Lauren and her sister must've taken after their mother. Joshua Caplan stood at about my height, his skin fair, and his eyes set in a permanent glare. If I didn't know anything about him, I got the feeling my instincts would still tell me not to trust him. He shouted again, outraged that I was even here.

"I'm asking you—who the hell let him through?"

The security guard shrunk under the boom of his entitled shouting. From the way that Caplan fumed, I got the sense that Lauren must've been close by. I walked pass the both of them, eyes scanning each door's window for signs of her. It was the rough snatch of hands, grabbing at the back of my hoodie that pulled me out of my mission, my back being slammed against a wall.

Joshua Caplan's hand circled around my neck, tight enough to convey a threat, but not enough to restrict my airway. I was exhausted, so even though I could've snapped his arm back and away from me, I didn't fight it. And perhaps, if there was still a Lauren to do this for, I didn't fight back because he was her father.

"You!" *Venomous* was the only word I had for his tone. "You did this to her."

Lauren once said '*The blame game is all about varying degrees of association. You can make anything anyone's fault if you look at situations from different directions*.' One way to look at things was this—Joshua Caplan could share in some of the blame. He certainly hadn't thought about her safety when he kicked her out of his house last month. I supposed his anger was not out of grief alone, but a desperation to not blame himself.

If only I could be so cognitively dissonant. I wished I could find a scapegoat to levy all my guilt upon. No, I knew what role I played in all of this, and so I nodded. *Yeah, I did do this to her*. This *was* my fault.

Caplan's grip around my neck tightened. "I could kill you right now."

He wasn't bluffing. I could see it in his eyes that he meant every word. And it scared me—not because I found Joshua Caplan particularly threatening. Nah, this nigga's hands were softer than his daughters. It scared me because my immediate thought after he threatened my life was, '*Hey, maybe that ain't such a bad idea.*'

But nah, Lauren wasn't dead yet, which meant I needed to carry this one out. No tap outs.

Evidently the lone security guard on this floor had called for backup, given the three new uniformed guards running up from behind Caplan.

My fingers tightened around his wrist, Lauren's blood still staining my fingernails, and I pulled his hand away from my neck. An angrier me would've broken his wrist for good measure, but I didn't need to do all of that. It would really upset Lauren if I did.

When I let Caplan go, of course he lunged for me again, this time only to be restrained by hospital security. There was outrage as he shouted—cursed at me, cursed at them.

"I'm the state's attorney for this district. Let me go or I will have all your fuckin' jobs."

It didn't surprise me at all that Caplan was the type to say shit like that to people. They ignored his threats, pulling him further away from where I stood.

To me, a security officer explained, "Sir, you need to leave this floor. You're not supposed to be here."

That warning told me that Lauren had to be here somewhere. I didn't budge. "I'm waiting for Dr. Montgomery-Bryce to get out of—"

"Dr. Montgomery-Bryce is out of the OR. If she's expecting you, I can escort you down to her office."

Resignedly, I shook my head. "I know where it is."

Chapter Fifteen

KAIN

She hadn't been expecting me, but she wasn't surprised when she found me at the other side of her door. I took this to mean that she's heard about what happened to Lauren.

Monique's eyes were sympathetic when she nodded me into her office. I didn't want her sympathy, though. I wanted answers. She waited until I sat down before taking her own seat behind a dark wood desk. I hardly got a word in before Monique huffed, her tone almost whiny.

"You know they didn't want me to operate on her at first? Her family, I mean."

That wasn't surprising at all. Adding her husband's last name to hers didn't make her any less of a Montgomery. And given the likely culprit behind Lauren's shooting, I could understand why Lauren's family wouldn't want Monique operating on their daughter.

"I'm the best emergency surgeon in this hospital, and they thought that I might want to, *'Finish what my father started.'* Can you believe that? How do they even know Daddy had something to do with this? Isn't he a thousand miles away, in Memphis, right now?"

"He did set it up," I pushed past this revelation quickly, eager to get to the point. "Silas said he was gonna make me watch her die. And it looks like he made good on that promise."

Monique had nothing to say to this. My sister, while in the dark about a lot of things pertaining to our father, was not stupid. If I said he was involved, it wouldn't be difficult for her to wrap her head around.

"Well…" She found it difficult to piece together her words, hesitant to tell me whatever it was. My anxiety fired up. "Well… because her family didn't want me in on the surgery, they had to call an off-duty surgeon in, half asleep and bleary-eyed."

I knew bad news was coming.

"He was heavy handed, puncturing her left side lung during the bullet removal." I leaned forward onto the edge of my seat. "I had to be called in to help last minute, and we couldn't fix it. What was supposed to be a simple bullet removal turned into a very complicated pneumonectomy."

"A what?"

"We had to remove one of her lungs. Her body is getting acclimated to the loss, and she can't breathe on her own right now. To make for an easier recovery, she's been induced into a coma, where she will stay until she learns to function efficiently with just the one lung."

I didn't even realize my eyes were watering until Monique reached across her desk and pulled a tissue loose. I declined the offer, clearing my throat before asking, "Can I see her?"

"Oh, Kain," she whispered softly, shaking her head, "You know I can't—"

"Please." I wasn't too proud to beg.

Monique sat back, drawing the tissue she'd offered earlier to her own eyes. "Kain, go home."

"*Monique*—"

"Kain, go home," she repeated, pushing out a frustrated sigh. "Go home, wash up, change out of your bloody clothes, and come back after visitation hours have closed—that's after ten o'clock—and... And I'll see what I can do."

July 31st, 2016, was the longest day of my life. After getting cleaned up, I sat in the parking lot of Jackson Memorial, watching the sky, very slowly, grow dark. The hours passed like years—a prison sentence of guilt, of depression, pure torture.

At exactly one minute after ten o'clock, I was sitting in the hospital lobby, just outside a gift shop where Monique had told me to wait. I thought about buying Lauren flowers, ultimately deciding against it because I knew I wouldn't be able to leave them with her. Every odd second or so, I checked the time on my wrist watch.

Monique was six minutes late, and after waiting several hours for this, each minute she wasted felt cruel.

It was her hand on my shoulder that snapped me out of whatever haze I'd zoned out into.

"Come on, follow me."

Maybe it was all in my head, but I could've sworn that as Monique lead me further and further into the back of the hospital, the air around me got colder. She stopped at a door, scanning around us for any prying eyes.

"I told the staff on this floor to give you some leeway. But I can't do anything about her family," Monique explained. "So as a favor to me, make sure you're out of this room before visitation begins tomorrow morning at eight o'clock. Please."

"You mean... You don't mind if I stay through the night?"

"I figured you might want to since—"

Without warning, I pulled my older sister into a hug, a silent thank you. On a day filled with so many disappointments, this opportunity was, as sad as it may seem, a silver lining. Monique held open the door nodding me in with a final reminder.

"Be out of this hospital by seven fifty-nine."

She shut the door behind me, leaving me in a room that was mostly dark aside from the bedside lamp off to the side of where Lauren lay. I followed the light, pulling a chair against the wall closer to the side of her bed, my eyes never once veering away from her face.

Lauren had been poked and prodded, tubes in her nose and mouth, breathing for her because she could no longer do it on her own.

My favorite thing about watching Lauren sleep was the way that she used to breathe, the rhythmic rise and fall of her chest used to be hypnotizing. And now, with the help of a machine, her breathing was now measured, mechanic in its timing. In and then out, a predictable beat that was all too unnatural.

I took a seat, my hand finding hers tucked under the sterile, white hospital sheets.

"Hey," I whispered, leaning forward and resting my head on the space left in the bed beside her. Her fingers were warm, an oddly comforting observation. Warmth meant that she was still alive. Even if there was a loud ass machine doing all the breathing for her, there was still something I could hold onto. All was not lost. She was still here.

So I spoke to her.

"I did some Googling online and read that patients on life support have a low probability of bein' able to hear things that are said to them, but there are some cases where they wake up, say they heard it, and remember it all."

I let my fingers caress the skin of the back of her hand. I might've hoped for a squeeze or a twitch of her fingers to give me some sign that she could hear me, but there was none of that. Still, I kept talking.

"Do you remember our first date? When I found out you get down with catfish?" I chuckled at the memory. "I remember tellin' you I don't like seafood, and you were outraged to hear it. I remember thinking to myself, *'What is she so outraged for? Catfish ain't seafood, it's lakefood.'*

"And then you said something along the lines of, why would I agree to go to a restaurant called Catfish

Carol's if I knew I wasn't tryna eat fish. I didn't say at the time, 'cause I thought it would've come off wild corny, but... I just wanted to see you again. Though, I felt that should've been obvious.

"Then there was the time we had that first self-defense lesson. There's this thing you used to do when I got real close—you'd hold your breath—and you thought I didn't notice. I did. I'd take one step back, and suddenly you were gasping for air. It was cute."

I sniffed, bringing the back of my free hand to my eyes. As comforting as it was to be here, to see her, that didn't make the view any less heartbreaking.

"Last night you asked me what I would do if I lost you, and I said I didn't know. No more than five hours later, I held you in my arms as you started to die, and for a brief moment, I caught a glimpse of exactly what I would do if I lost you. It felt like a piece of me just... broke. I got numb, and the sounds around me grew muffled. I just...separated. It was like I stepped away from the scene and was looking at myself from further away. Nothin' felt real, and so in turn, nothin' felt like it mattered."

I thought I hit rock bottom the night Amir died.
Nope.

Evidently, there were still a million more miles I could fall.

"I think I might do the therapy thing." I swiped a thumb across the backs of her fingers, a little consoled by the feel of her hand in mine. "Actually, I'll bargain with you. If you make a full and speedy recovery, I will do whatever you want. Just start breathing on your own."

Despite the intrusive beeping that sounded off from the machines keeping her alive, when I laid my head back down on the space that she left, sleep eventually did come. Even in a coma, Lauren's presence still put my heart at ease.

When I woke the following morning, the sun was beginning to creep up and into the sky. I looked at the watch on my wrist, noting that I didn't have much time. Reluctantly letting go of her hand, I rose to my feet, brushing her hair away from her forehead before saying goodbye with a parting kiss.

"I'll be back later," I whispered against her hair—a promise. "I love you."

And I did come back that night.

And the next night.

And the next.

Chapter Sixteen

KAIN

Silas was extradited out of Memphis.

After Lauren was shot, her best friend, Lux, came forward. Lux revealed to the media that Lauren's life had been threatened by Silas back in March, as an attempt to deter Joshua Caplan's investigation. Because of Lux's accusations, which could be backed up with text messages she shared with Lauren, it wasn't long before Silas was charged for possible involvement in the shooting, being held in custody with no bail. When Lux was asked by reporters why Lauren never went to the police, she turned her wrath to me.

"Kain told her he would protect her... And she stupidly believed him."

It wasn't before long that blogs began to speculate that my relationship with Lauren had been a setup all along. I was accused of taking advantage of her naiveté to gain her trust, build a relationship, and ultimately betray her. The media latched on to the theory and ran with it, running photos of Lauren and I being seen together at the beginning of the summer, in the days after Amir's funeral when we didn't care about being seen. I was made to look like a predator. It was sick.

But it got sicker.

Soon enough, the whole family was entrenched in some murder scheme against Lauren and her father, cooked up by insane YouTube conspiracy theorists, connecting dots that weren't there. Sanaa was accused of setting up my birthday party at *The Diamond Palace* so that Silas would know where Lauren was that night. Monique was accused of trying to botch Lauren's lifesaving surgery, getting blamed for the mistake that the first surgeon made—the mistake that caused Lauren to lose one of her lungs and get put on life support.

I was the bait. Sanaa was the net. And Monique was the slaughter. The only person whose name wasn't being dragged through the mud was Cierra's.

These online bloggers made Silas out to be some criminal mastermind with his evil children in tow. And for what? So Joshua Caplan could be taught a lesson? That didn't even make any sense. My sister, Cierra, seemed to come out of hiding for the sole purpose of fanning the flames, posting cryptic and subliminal Tweets that alluded to the fact that she hoped Lauren would die. Cierra was angry at Sanaa for befriending Lauren, angry with me for being the reason Amir was dead, so she was making it worse on purpose.

It didn't look good.

Though none of the accusations levied by online commentators would ever hold up in court, the court of public opinion was destroying my sisters' lives.

Silas, to my surprise, released a statement through his lawyer that said he had nothing to do with Lauren's shooting. It was out of character for him, as I'd never known Silas to publicly deny anything through an attorney. Perhaps he felt like this new accusation was going to hurt his upcoming trial. Although the case he was going to court for and Lauren's shooting were unrelated charges, it was obvious that his official statement was used in order to keep him from looking even more guilty. There was no way the jurors on his upcoming trial didn't have pre-trial opinions of him now. His alleged involvement in Lauren's shooting had branched out of local Miami news and was now being covered nationally.

Silas was fucked.

Whether or not he won this upcoming case didn't matter.

When it came to Lauren's shooting, he wasn't going to be able to finesse his way out of this charge. With Lauren's best friend swearing up and down that Silas was the culprit to any reporter who gave her a mic, it just wasn't looking good for him.

I kept the news on in Lauren's room as I watched the latest updates on my family. I hadn't seen anyone in my family, except for Monique, since my birthday party. I'd been staying at Marlon's since he lived very close to the hospital. I never wanted to be too far away in case Lauren woke up.

It was a little after eleven at night, day five since Lauren's shooting, and as usual she was lying motionless in bed, the beeping of her breathing machine so loud that I needed to put subtitles up on the TV.

"Remember the night we met and I told you I didn't think Silas was gonna lose the case your father's been building against him?" Of course she didn't answer. "Well..." I shut off the TV. "...I still don't think Silas is going to lose that case. Still no witnesses. But this new case involving you? He doesn't a stand a chance with that one."

"There are now *two* people who have come forward and said Silas wanted you killed. Your best friend, Lux, and some nigga with one arm, named Swiss. It took me a while to remember where I knew that name from— *Swiss*. And then I remembered... That's the dude you shot that night those other two niggas brought you over to the house." I shook my head at the irony.

"Yeah... He was on *Good Morning America*, touting himself as a reformed criminal who saw the light the night his friends kidnapped you for Silas. Said he wanted no parts, and got out of the car. Lyin' ass nigga, just lookin' to get something outta the situation 'cause he thinks his friends double-crossed him... Still, he basically confirmed to the world that Silas *did* have a bounty out for you."

"Silas might win the trial coming up, but there's no way he's winning this next one," I assured her. "He'll pay for what he did to you."

* * *

I woke up to the smell of blood.

Immediately my head snapped up, my hands in an alarmed frenzy as I reached for the light beside Lauren's bed. The night table clock informed me that it was a little after five o'clock in the morning. I had just under three hours left until regular visitation kicked in, and I would have to leave.

With the help of her machine, Lauren was still breathing, and her skin was still warm to the touch. I breathed out a sigh of relief, thankful to know the worst was avoided. Still, I searched for the source of the smell, troubled by even the thought that Lauren was bleeding somewhere, no matter how harmless it might be.

"Baby, I'm just gonna check your stitches," I explained, just in case she could feel a draft from me rising the covers off her body. Carefully, I drew up her hospital gown, doing my best not to touch the healing bruises along her side.

My breath stopped for a moment. Not because I'd found the source of the bleeding, but because this was the first time I was seeing the operation wound, a long and curved stitch running along her ribcage, a heartbreaking imperfection on what used to be flawless brown skin. Just looking at it, I already knew she was going to hate the scarring.

This would forever be a constant reminder of her ordeal. Lauren would never be able to look at her own body without horrifying flashbacks. *Fuck*, I thought to myself, a pang of guilt shooting through me. I felt pins and needles in the backs of my eyes as I drew the gown down.

Things like this aren't supposed to happen to people like her.

Still, the smell of blood in the air persisted, and so I had to continue to look for the source. When I drew the blanket back completely and searched a little harder, I found it. A small red stain between her legs.

I don't think I'd ever been so relieved to find out someone was on their period. Releasing a sigh, I drew the covers back and pulled my phone out from my back pocket.

Monique picked up after the first ring.

"Hey, Mo," I said tiredly into the receiver, walking away from Lauren so, in case she actually could hear me, I wouldn't make her feel embarrassed. "Is there someone you can send up to get Lauren cleaned up? She just got her period."

"Her period?"

"Yeah, I checked under the covers. There's blood between her legs."

"I see." My sister's voice got lower. "Sit tight, I'll be right up with a nurse."

That seemed like a bit much for a cleanup job, but it had been hours since anyone had come up to check on Lauren, so she was kind of overdue for a check on her vitals. When the door to Lauren's room opened, Monique walked in with an older nurse, a fresh gown in her hands. I didn't have to be told that I needed to step out while my sister and the nurse worked on Lauren. I was already on my way out.

I waited outside, eyes on the watch on my wrist, waiting for them to finish up. They were taking longer than I expected. When the door behind me finally opened, I turned to find Monique standing there, her eyes sympathetically looking up at me as the nurse she came up with excused herself.

"Is something wrong?" I read her expression, slightly alarmed. "Is something wrong with Lauren?"

"No," Monique assured softly, something still off in her demeanor. "*Lauren* is fine. Well... she's in the same condition"

Her emphasis on Lauren's name rubbed me the wrong way, as if even though Lauren was unchanged, something had definitely occurred. Lauren, as far as I knew, was the only person in that room. I looked at my sister expectantly, wordlessly asking her to explain her strange behavior.

"Kain, it wasn't my place to tell you..." Monique leaned against the back wall, her usual doctor seriousness cast aside for a bit. She was hurting. Whatever it was that she couldn't tell me before, it was hurting her now. "I thought if Lauren woke up—"

"*When*," I corrected.

"Right," Monique nodded. "I thought *when* Lauren woke up, she might want to tell you herself, so it wasn't my place to say anything. God, Kain... Lauren didn't get her period just now..." My instincts kicked in before she could say it. I didn't know until that moment—or maybe it was that I had missed every warning sign, and in that moment, they all resurfaced. Monique didn't need to say the words, because somehow before she said them, flashbacks of the past seven weeks hit me at once—and I figured it out on my own, just before Monique said the words. "...she had a miscarriage."

Chapter Seventeen

KAIN

I consider myself to be an observant person. I tend to pick up on things people usually miss, and I might've picked up the clues that Lauren left this summer if I hadn't been wrapped up in my own depression bullshit.

Seven weeks. She was seven weeks along.

What was I doing seven weeks ago?

I was buying *Plan B* at a pharmacy with Lauren. She'd read the box at least a dozen times, saying something or another about articles she'd read about side effects. I'd said something dismissive, telling her it definitely wouldn't happen again. I think I might've been short with her, visibly irritated at the time. She'd excused herself to get a glass of water from the kitchen.

But I never actually saw her take the pill.

She was so insecure about our relationship at the beginning of the summer. I could actually imagine why she would try to get pregnant on purpose. Maybe she thought that would keep me with her. She wasn't convinced that she had me then.

Lauren had a glow about her all summer, and I thought it was because she was happy. I'd spent six weeks with Lauren, a woman, and was never shown any sign that she was on her period even once.

I could recall her eagerness to see my baby pictures, how she gushed over them for days after getting them.

When Lauren showed up at my doorstep at the beginning of the summer, she was at least ten pounds lighter than I remembered her. Six weeks pass, and she gained it all back, plus a little more. I chalked it off as eating well.

I remembered thinking it was strange that she was drinking Sprite the night of my birthday. If I wasn't mistaken, she'd actually said the words, '*No alcohol for me.*' I remember thinking it was odd that she had spent all that time planning the evening, only to turn around and refuse to have at least one drink during. I'd chalked that off as some sort of leftover issue from that night she almost got raped.

And finally, the biggest sign of them all—that same night, in the champagne room. I didn't have a condom, and Lauren barely hesitated when she told me, '*It doesn't matter.*'

How did I not see it?

How *the fuck* did I not see it?

It was creeping into noon, way past the time I should have left. I sat at Lauren's bedside, unwilling to leave her now in the wake of this bombshell, my head resting lightly on her stomach. She looked so frail to me now, the rise and fall of her chest still frustratingly unnatural. Tears, which I'd grown used to (and tired of) in the past several days, flowed more freely now than they ever had.

"Did you think I was gonna get mad at you if you told me?" My voice was just below a whisper. It didn't matter. She wouldn't hear me even if I shouted. "I'm not mad. I promise. And I'm not just sayin' this because you're in a coma, either."

I took her by the hand, resting her fingers along the side of my cheek.

"You could've told me… You could've told me day one if you didn't want to take the *Plan B*. I swear I wouldn't have forced you to. I might've just tried to explain that you didn't need to do it to keep me. Baby, you've had me since the night we first met."

"And if you still didn't want to take the *Plan B*, then we could've dealt with all of this together. You didn't have to hold onto this on your own for so long. I'm sorry if I made you feel like you couldn't talk to me."

When Lauren was shot, finding out that she'd survived made me feel like I'd narrowly escaped the worst. And now…

"Can I tell you something?" I whispered quietly. "I don't really go around telling women this, 'cause if you say it out loud, it kinda seems like you're askin' for something. But… I've always wanted a huge family. I mean, I already *have* a huge family, but what I mean is, a family of my own. I guess what I'm tryna let you know is that if you'd told me sooner, it would've been nothin' for me to start getting used to the idea. I wouldn't have been upset at all."

"Especially not upset with you. Especially you... 'Cause you mean the world to me, Lauren." I raised the back of my hand to my eyes, feeling as though I'd been kicked in the stomach when I said the words, "You *both* would've meant the world to me."

Behind my head, cutting into the silence, I heard a throat clear. I cringed, not having heard the door, and because the sound was distinctively male. I wasn't ready to say goodbye to her. I didn't want to leave.

But it would only be a short time before Joshua Caplan called security. I rose my head from Lauren's stomach, running my hands down my face before standing to face the man behind me.

"That was heartfelt."

I couldn't tell if he was mocking me, but I wasn't in the mood for a conversation. Especially not one with him. So I ignored it, wordlessly brushing passed his shoulders on my way to the door.

"I didn't say you had to leave." My hand froze at the knob, and I looked over my shoulder to confirm I'd heard him correctly. "They told me downstairs that she lost *it*."

Evidently, Lauren's pregnancy was known about by everyone except for me.

It.

I didn't like his word choice. I didn't like anything about this man. I was caught between a strong desire to stay with Lauren, but an overwhelming urge to get as far from her father as I could. Caplan had such a punchable face. The type of face that practically begged to be smashed in, features wrought with an overstated sense of confidence, and just a generally untrustworthy energy.

Oddly enough, he kind of reminded me of Silas.

When I didn't say anything, he continued to speak. "I don't understand how you can stand there and pine after her, mourn the loss of your child, and still do *nothing*."

"What?"

"Your father," he expressed pointedly, irritated that I hadn't caught on immediately. "He's the reason my daughter is in this hospital bed, on *life support*. He's the reason *your* son or daughter is dead. He's taken something from both of us, if not more from you."

"Y'all extradited him out of Memphis less than twenty-four hours after Lauren was shot," I reminded. "What? You expect me to singlehandedly break into the prison, and kill him there?"

"Kill him," Caplan scoffed with a shake of his head. "That's all you people deal in, huh? Street justice. A life for a life. Like animals."

If I thought Caplan had a punchable face before, that slick ass mouth only served to strengthen the urge. I glanced at Lauren as she slept in her hospital bed, a reminder that no matter how much I wanted to, I could not touch her father. Even the worst people have kids who love them.

"Do it the right way. Do it the legal way—legal justice," Caplan urged. "For her."

"You gotta be a little more specific."

"I'm bringing your father's case to trial the day after tomorrow, and I don't have any witnesses taking the stand. You and I both know your father doesn't trust anyone as much as he trusts you, so—"

"No. Can't help you."

Caplan's shoulders squared up. He cut the bullshit indoor voice, angrily shouting, "You would let him walk? After what he did to Lauren?"

"I'm not lettin' him do anything. Silas is being held in the state pen without bail over Lauren's shooting. He might beat *your* case this week, but when he's taken to trial over what happened to *her*, it's a done deal regardless. Silas ain't gonna walk for this."

"I don't want him to beat my case."

"What difference does it make to me? Your case ain't even about Lauren. I don't owe you shit."

I knew what this was.

For years, Caplan had fantasized about being the prosecutor who would bring Silas down. I wouldn't have been surprised to learn it was what he thought about while he fucked his wife. And now, Silas was on the chopping block for two crimes against the state. The case Lauren's father would be trying was sure to lose. After all, he had no witnesses.

The second case—the one about Lauren—that would be the one that would get Silas sent away for good. At Silas' age and health status, any prison sentence over twenty years was a life sentence. In the state of Florida, conspiracy to commit murder was twenty-five years.

Silas was going down for this. The evidence was stacked against him.

But because Lauren was his daughter, it was guaranteed that Caplan wouldn't be able to prosecute the second case. Personal connections to the victim are automatic disqualifiers for prosecutors. But Caplan, ever the egotistical one, couldn't be satisfied to know that Silas was going to see *"legal justice"*. Not if he wasn't going to get the credit for it, not if his name wasn't in the law history books. He coveted that legacy. That was clear.

Caplan was a real piece of work. Did he think I was too dumb to realize what his angle was?

"She'll get her justice," I assured, reaching for the door handle. "You, on the other hand—I could give a fuck about your legacy."

Just short of me stepping out, Caplan barked, "You think she'll be around to see it?"

I stopped dead in my tracks. Sure I'd misheard what he just said, I had to ask.

"What'd you just say to me?"

"Her justice," Caplan explained impatiently. "Do you think she'll be around to see it?"

I shut the door behind me, stepping further into the room. I knew exactly what Lauren's father was trying to say, but I still couldn't believe it. "Are you threatening me?"

"Threatening you?" he repeated back at me incredulously. "Of course not, Kain. It's just that... Lauren's been on life support for almost two weeks; no sign of improvement. Every day she spends in this hospital bed, she amasses tens of thousands of dollars in bills. If I know how legal timelines work—and trust me, I do—then your father probably won't be brought to trial for her shooting for at least another two years. A year and a half, if we're lucky. And I just wonder how much longer I can afford this. A month? A year? Two years? What do I look like? A millionaire? Lately I've been feeling like every day is much too high of an expense."

This man is a fuckin' monster.

"If you don't want to pay for it, then I will," I offered.

"Oh noo, I don't want your money, kid," Caplan declined, taking a step back and caressing his sleeping daughter's cheek. He rose his gaze to meet my eyes. "I just want you to take the stand. What do you say?"

Chapter Eighteen

KAIN

Caplan wasted no time telling the press that I'd been vetted as a witness.

When the story broke the following day, my sister Petra, all the way in Memphis, called me twenty-eight times. Monique called me forty-three times. Sanaa called me fifty-six times. Even Cierra broke her summer-long silence, and called me twice.

My uncle Vance took home the gold medal, calling me a total of one hundred and six times.

I didn't pick up a single call because I knew what they would say.

Kain, you can't do this.

But they didn't understand.

I had to.

I paced aimlessly in the living room of Marlon's home. My phone vibrated on the coffee table. It was late, a little after four AM. Caplan's trial against Silas was starting in four hours or so. Even if I wanted to, I wouldn't have been able to sleep.

Never in a million years, no matter how much I hated Silas, did I ever envision myself testifying against him in court. And these feelings did not arise out of some deep seeded love or loyalty for Silas. Stuff like this was just the kind of thing you'd rather die than do in my world.

On the street, the worst thing anyone could possibly be was a snitch. To get on the stand at anyone's trial and publicly point fingers—that was the worst kind. I might've been signing my own death certificate in signing up for this. But if I didn't, I knew for a fact I'd be signing hers.

If Lauren had been unable to hear me speak to her all this time, then I was happy she didn't have to hear her father leverage her life just to win a *fucking* case.

Another two hours passed, and my stress level rose as the trial drew closer. I was already dressed to sit on the stand—the same suit I'd worn to Amir's funeral. *You have to do this.* I repeated that fact in my head at least a hundred times. *You have to do this. You have to do this. You have to do this.*

My mantra was interrupted by a banging at Marlon's door. It was six o'clock in the morning so I was sure he slept through it. The banging persisted.

"Youngblood! Youngblood!"

Vance.

He would bang and shout the whole neighborhood awake if I didn't open that door. I knew he was going to try to talk me out of the decision I'd made. Not for Silas' sake, but for mine. If I seriously took the stand against Silas, my own father, my reputation out here was as good as trashed.

But Vance didn't understand.

I had to.

"I know why you're doing this." My uncle was breathless, eyes bloodshot like he hadn't slept. I wondered which of my sisters had given him Marlon's address. He pushed pass me, and into the house.

"No you don't," was all I could say.

"You're doing it for her!" *Okay, maybe he did know.* "Because Silas tried to kill her."

No, because her own father threatened to kill her if I didn't. I didn't bother explaining myself. It didn't even sound believable out loud.

"But Silas didn't do it!" Vance practically shouted, eyes crazy. "Silas did not try to kill her."

"Vance, I don't have time for this…"

"No! LISTEN TO ME!" He grabbed at my shoulders, his touch confrontational and angry. "Your father released an official statement—"

"Yeah, I read it. It was bullshit."

"No. NO! Listen to me, Kain! Tell me—when have you ever known Silas to publicly deny anything through an attorney? Especially if he did it?"

"I imagine he might do it when there's actual damning evidence against him," I guessed, not caring to know the motivation behind my father's out of character behavior.

"I'm telling you, it wasn't Silas. I've been talkin' to him since they arrested him for it. He told me himself that he didn't order that hit."

"You sure about that shit, Vance? Silas promised me that he would make sure I watched Lauren die. I don't understand why you tryna fight me on this. He basically made good on his promise."

I checked the time on my watch. The clock was ticking. Soon I would need to head out for court before morning traffic hit.

"Something about this whole situation ain't felt right since day one, and I know you feel it. You smart, Youngblood. Don't let your grief make you stupid. Think!"

Luck.

I've never believed in luck. When Lauren was shot, I'd be lying if I didn't say I was surprised to have only heard one gunshot. Lauren was shot only once by an unseen gunman who fled the scene before he could confirm the kill. How lucky.

"Alright." I acknowledged that, yes, maybe something hadn't felt right since day one. "What am I missing?"

"I think you know."

"Let's say I don't."

Vance shook his head and explained, "I saw the way you shot that man that night you killed those niggas that brought Lauren to the house. You shoot just like your father, you know that? Right between the eyebrows."

"Where is this going?"

"Did he teach you how to kill people, Kain? Or did you just see him do it enough times for you to teach yourself how it's done?" I didn't answer the question, and Vance tried to make his point. "You know your father better than anyone, Kain. And you know where he likes his targets to be shot."

Vance came in closer, sleep deprived eyes on me analytically as he stepped around where I stood.

"Your girl was shot right here, am I right?" He pressed his finger to my side, digging into my ribcage. "So that's what? A shot to the lung at worst? So what's one lung? People got two a' those. A real hitta would've never left the scene for a single shot to the ribs."

"You think whoever shot Lauren wasn't tryna kill her," I guessed.

Vance shook his head. "No, that's not what I'm saying at all."

I looked at him questioningly.

"All I'm saying is this—if Silas ordered that hit, she wouldn't be on life support, she'd be dead. A shot to the ribs is nothing to drive away over. You know that. I know that. And anybody Silas would've put to the task would have known that."

"Lauren doesn't have enemies like that."

Vance tilted his head to the side, squinting a little when he replied, "But I'm sure *you* do."

I wracked my brain for possible suspects. I could only really think of one other person in my life who might want Lauren dead. "Cierra ain't about that life."

"Really, nigga?" Vance was frustrated. "Ain't no way you grew up with Silas and turned out this naïve. Of course it wasn't Cierra! That's obvious! Did you even watch the surveillance footage from that night? It's on YouTube."

"I watched it once." Only once, and that was it. I didn't really enjoy reliving the experience. "The only people in the frame are Lauren and I. All you can see is the part where Lauren is shot. No visible gunman."

"I think you need to watch it again."

Vance pulled out his phone before I could decline, pulling up the video on screen.

It was a five second clip. In the video, just as I remembered, I turned around to tell Lauren to walk where I could see her, sidestepping so that she could walk ahead. And then she was shot.

Vance played the video again.

And again.

And again.

And again.

"Do you see what I see?" he asked. "Lemme play it again and narrate for you." He pressed play. "Here you two are laughing, you turn, step out of the way, she's hit." He pressed play again. "Again, you turn and step out of the way, and she's immediately hit. You step out of the way. She's hit. You step out of the way. She's hit."

Vance was actually beginning to make sense. So much sense, that I lost my words.

"So, if you see what I see, then that means you realize that if the gunman was aiming for Lauren, then they had a terrific sense of timing. Crazy that a person with such a sharp eye for timing didn't use that eye to aim for a kill shot. Unless…"

"They weren't aiming for her," I surmised.

Vance clapped once, pointing in my direction.

"I understand that your girl was shot, and that shit fucked with you, so you wasn't really paying attention to details like that. But for days, I've done nothing *but* think about the details. Who would want you dead, Kain?

I thought about the eyes glaring at me at Amir's funeral. "Shit... a lot of people."

Vance shook his head. "You not thinking hard enough. Let me break down these questions. Who would want *you* dead, accidentally shoot Lauren, and then flee the scene? Why not shoot you both? Who fires only one bullet when a handgun holds at least six?"

Who fires only one bullet when a handgun holds at least six?

I automatically knew the answer to that question.

"Someone who panics."

"And which one of your enemies would panic after accidentally shooting Lauren, when they meant to shoot you? Because, objectively speaking, if I wanted you dead and I accidentally shot your girl, I would just shoot you next. Two bodies instead of one—oh fuckin' well." Vance stared at me pointedly. "But whoever accidentally shot your girl, had to immediately give up on tryna kill *you*, because... Well, shit, *somebody* had to call an ambulance for her."

Vance watched me carefully as I put together the pieces, finally beginning to see the bigger picture. Without saying anything, I knew what Vance was trying to get me to figure out, and now that I knew...it all made sense.

"After Amir's funeral, you and Lauren must've showed up in about a dozen news stories, being seen together like some Miami version of Romeo and Juliette. House Montgomery falling in love with House Caplan—

the media ate that shit up. There was a local news segment every night for almost two weeks. You had to have known that shit was pissing off her father, tarnishing his good image. Shit, if it were my daughter, I would have tried to kill you, too.

"Except, he accidentally shoots his own daughter, decided to let your father take the blame, and now is using your grief to his benefit. Making the best of a fucked up situation that he made. I told you that Caplan was ruthless, Youngblood. All about his numbers."

What was initially shock was beginning to subside. For the first time in a while, my hands began to feel hot. The way they only got when I felt the burgeoning of an uncontrollable anger. Thinking about the way Caplan had threatened to cut off Lauren's life support, when he knew full well he was the reason she was there… The corners of my vision started to blur into black. I wasn't just angry. I wanted to hurt somebody.

"Do you know how Romeo and Juliette ends? I read it in prison. It was actually kinda sad. So as the war between House Montague and House Capulet raged on, because she wanted to be with Romeo, Juliette drinks an elixir that will make everybody think she's dead, but she's really only sleeping. But the bitch forgot to tell Romeo that. So Romeo is fucked up over the news of her death, rushes to her bedside and swallows a poison—suicide— dying seconds before wakes up. When Juliette wakes up, she finds him dead. She takes Romeo's knife, and stabs herself in the stomach. No happy ending."

I was only half listening to what Vance was saying now. The trial was set to start in an hour, and as a witness on the stand, I was going to have to be there. In my world, testifying in court was something you only did if you had a death wish—suicide. Even still, court was the one place I knew Caplan would be.

And whether I testified or not, court was where I was going.

The FINAL book in the series (When Souls Collide) is NOW AVAILABLE in the AMAZON booktore!

Please be sure to follow Millie Belizaire on Amazon! (pretty please)

ALSO FOLLOW ME ON...

Facebook

Instagram

Twitter

Made in the USA
Columbia, SC
28 November 2024

47788298R00121